Wendelin Van Draanen

SWEAR
TO
HOWDY

Alfred A. Knopf   New York

THIS IS A BORZOI BOOK PUBLISHED BY ALFRED A. KNOPF

KNOPF, BORZOI BOOKS, and the colophon are registered trademarks
of Random House, Inc.

www.randomhouse.com/kids

Library of Congress Cataloging-in-Publication Data

Van Draanen, Wendelin.
Swear to howdy / Wendelin Van Draanen. — 1st ed.
p.   cm.
Summary: Two thirteen-year-old boys share neighborhood adventures, complaints
about their older sisters, family secrets, and even guilt that bind them together in
a special friendship.
ISBN 0-375-82505-3 (trade) — ISBN 0-375-92505-8 (lib. bdg.)
[1. Friendship—Fiction.   2. Brothers and sisters—Fiction.
3. Family problems—Fiction.]   I. Title.
PZ7.V2857Sw 2003
[Fic]—dc21
2002043442

Printed in the United States of America

October 2003

10 9 8 7 6 5 4 3 2 1

First Edition

Also by Wendelin Van Draanen

To Arlen, with love

I'd like to thank:
my Southern belles,
Susan Huffman, Mary Marshall Jones, and Becky Young,
for their help with this book
as well as
Ann Scott, Marquita Self, and Cindy Cason,
for showing me what Southern hospitality is all about;
my sons' scoutmaster Rodney McGuire, who joined the "Lord's
bouquet" much too early but who will be remembered for his
generous heart and warm Southern spirit;
my editor, Nancy Siscoe, for not thinking I'm crazy;
my husband, Mark Parsons, who knows that I am
but loves me anyway.

CONTENTS

1
CRAPPIES BITE

Joey's blood got mixed up in mine the same way mine got mixed up in his. Drop by drop. Pact by pact. And there's times that makes me feel good, but there's times it creeps me out. Reminds me.

Seems like Joey and me were always making pacts. Lots of pacts, leading up to that last one. "Rusty," he'd say to me. "I swear to howdy, if you tell a soul . . ."

"I won't!" I'd tell him. "I swear!" Then he'd put out his fist and we'd go through the ritual, hammering fists and punching knuckles. And after we'd nicked fingers and mixed blood he'd heave a sigh and say, "You're a true friend, Rusty-boy," and that'd be that. Another secret, sealed for life.

Joey's family moved to Lost River two years before we did, so Pickett Lane was his turf, and that was just fine by me. Especially since he was so cool about it the summer we came to live next door. "Russell *Cooper?*" he'd asked me, and I'd thought, Oh man. Here we go again. Cooper-pooper. Pooper-scooper. I get the same old thing, everywhere I go.

But then he grinned at me the way only Joey Banks could grin, with one side of his face looped way up, and teeth showing everywhere. He nodded. "Rusty. That's what we'll call ya."

"Huh?"

"Don't stand there looking at me like a load of bricks, boy. You ain't never gonna survive around here with a name like Russell."

I must have been blinking but good, 'cause he slapped me across the face, *whap-whap*. Not hard or anything. Just playful-like. Then he waved me along, saying, "C'mon, Rusty. I'll show you around."

He tore down to the river, and I tore right after him. "This here's *my* hole," he said when we got to a side pool with tree branches hanging over it and rocks nearly clear around. "And nobody else better get caught swimmin' in it." He gave me that loopy grin again. "Nobody but me and you."

I almost said, "Me?" 'cause I couldn't believe my ears. It was the coolest pool I'd ever seen. There was a thick rope for swinging, and the rocks were flat and great for sunning. Not the kind of place that's easy to share. 'Specially with a stranger.

But I bit my tongue and filled my pocket with rocks like he was doing, then scrambled up the tree behind him. And when we were perched nice and steady, he started skipping rocks across the river, saying, "Let's see your arm, Rusty. How far can you hurl?"

Not as far as him, that's for sure. Especially since I had the wobbles, way up in that tree. But I chucked them as good as I could, and every time one plopped in the water, Joey'd say, "Nice one, Rusty! You're gettin' it!" Then he'd chuck one of his own nearly clear to the other shore.

When we were out of rocks, he started snapping off sticks. "Here, Rusty. Do like this," he told me, peeling leaves off. "Then shoot it in like . . ." He let it fly like a dart. "Watch it now . . . crappies pop up and snag 'em sometimes."

"Crappies do? You get 'em out here?"

He laughed. "Yep. Dad says they're lost, and I don't doubt it. Dumbest fish known to man. You can catch 'em with your thumb—if you got the nerve."

"You done that?" I asked him.

Snap went another twig, and he shot it in. "More'n once." He eyed me. "Hurts like hell." We watched the twig land and sail downstream. "They're good eatin', though. Man, they're tasty."

But the crappies weren't biting. Not at twigs, anyway. So after a spell Joey said, "Up for a swim, Rusty?"

"Now?" It was getting dark. Cooling off quick.

"Any time's good," he laughed. "Water's always just right."

He yanked off his shirt and his shoes and flung them down to shore. Then came the socks, *fling, fling*. And with a little scoot forward he grabbed the rope and said, "It's a blast, Rust, trust me."

"You goin' in like that?" I asked, looking at his jeans.

"I ain't gonna drown, if that's what you're worried about." He pulled up the rope, then backed along his branch, getting ready. "And I ain't gettin' down to my skivvies in front of you." He pushed off and swung out over the water, hollerin', "We only just met!"

Mama and Dad were none too pleased to see me soaked to the gills when I got home. And Sissy told me I looked like a drowned muskrat, then went back to painting her toes. But I ate like a horse and yapped like a terrier through supper, and everyone was surprised 'cause Mama claims I'm given to "quiet brooding."

So the next day, they let me go again. And the next, too. And the day after that. And before long Joey and me were swinging doubles and bombing each other in the pool, wearing nothing but skivvies and big fat grins.

We'd catch frogs and launch them into the river, too. Joey'd call, "Come 'n' get it!" to the crappies, but pretty much the frogs would just swim for a bit with their legs all sprawled, then go under on their own. And maybe it doesn't seem too exciting, doing this stuff day after day, but I had more fun in that single summer than I'd had in my entire life combined.

Then one day it was hotter'n Hades and we were hanging out on a big, flat rock after a swim, talking about how just the *thought* of middle school starting up was enough to spoil the last few days of summer—never mind all the fussin' your mama insisted on doin' to get you ready—when Joey let out the biggest, nastiest gasser you can imagine. My eyes bugged clear out and he laughed. "So let's hear what *you* got, Rusty-boy."

"Nothing like that," I told him. "Nothin' even close."

"Ha!" he said. "Let me teach ya."

"Teach me . . . ? To *fart?*"

He laughed again, then stuck his behind right up in the air. "First you get like this . . ."

"Joey, honest. I know how to fart."

"On command?"

"Well, no . . . depends on what I've been eating. Like if I've been eatin' *cabbage*—"

"Cabbage? Shoot, Rusty, you don't need to eat vile stuff to make righteous farts. Watch."

He got comfy on his elbows and knees, then bowed his head and hoisted his butt. And after a minute, he flipped around and let out the nastiest juicer I'd ever heard.

5

He laughed when he saw my face. "It's just *air*, Rusty-boy. Just air." He flipped around again. "Here, come on. Give it a shot."

"Nah . . ."

"Give it a *shot*."

"All right, all right!"

So I stuck my skivvies sky-high and waited. For what I wasn't real sure. And while Joey was flipping back and forth tootin' and hootin', I was propped up backward, feeling like one dumb fool.

"Nothin'?" he asked me finally.

I shook my head.

"You gotta relax."

I was about to tell him I'd practice at home, when he charged down the rock to the pool, yelling, "Ya gotta watch this!" He jumped into the water, then waited until the surface was calm. "Ready?" he called.

"Sure," I called back, glad to have my behind back where it belonged.

He held a finger up, his eyes big and bright, but all that happened was a couple of bubbles rolled to the surface.

"Shoot!" he said with a frown. "Too much interference!"

He climbed up to shore, stuck his butt up right there on the bank, then faced me and said, "Turn around."

So I turned away while he peeled out of his shorts. And when he'd waded out a safe distance, he sat down in the water and called, "Okay, *now* look!" Then he stuck a finger up in the air like he had before and waited. Only instead of gas bubbles coming to the surface, *he* came shooting out of the water like a torpedo, screaming like he was gonna die.

And then I saw it—a flashy, silvery, spiky-finned crappie chompin' down on his privates.

"Do something! *Do* something!" Joey screamed, flailing around, falling in the water, standing up, falling down, while that crappie hung on like it had struck the mother lode.

I didn't know how I was going to help, but I jumped in the pool anyway. But by the time I'd made it over to him,

Joey had stuck a finger through that crappie's gill and set himself free.

I tried not to look, but Joey was red, boy. Red and raw. He hurled the crappie way up onshore, then eased back into the water, whimpering and quivering, his eyes brimming with tears.

"You want me to get a doctor?" I whispered.

"No!"

"Did he . . . did he *get* any of it?"

"No!"

I stood there just waiting while he tried to ease the pain. But finally I couldn't help looking around the pond and asking, "What if there's *more* of 'em?"

He shot out of the water and dived for shore, holding himself safe the whole time. And after I'd left him alone to inspect himself for a minute, I tried asking again, "You sure you don't want to go to the doctor?"

He stepped into his skivvies and tucked himself away real careful-like before putting on his jeans. "No. What would he *do* to it, huh? I don't want no doctor bandaging me." Then he put on his shirt and said, "I swear to howdy, if you ever tell a soul . . ."

"I won't!"

His eyes squinted down on me. "I know how it goes. Especially when you start meetin' kids at school." He took a few painful steps, muttering, "And boy, this would be one temptin' tale to tell."

"I won't, Joey. I swear."

He checked my face over a minute while he tried to figure a new way to walk. "So we got a pact then?"

I nodded. "Sure."

"'Cause you know, you can't break no pact. It's a-moral."

"I won't tell, Joey. I swear."

He put out his fist, so I did, too. Then we hammered and punched each other's fists some, but he still wasn't sure we'd sealed the deal. So he dug up his pocketknife, sliced his finger, and looked at me while a drop of blood rose through his skin.

I put out my finger to prove I was good for his trust, and after he'd nicked it we put our fingers together and let the blood mix.

"You're a true friend, Rusty," he told me. "A true friend."

Then we took that crappie to Joey's house and fried it to a crisp. I didn't want any of it—couldn't seem to shake the thought of where it'd been—but Joey seemed to like it fine.

Ate the whole thing right up.

2

DIAMOND DOLL REVENGE

Joey's family and mine were alike in a lot of ways. Both our dads worked at the paper mill, both our mamas were helpers at schools—Mrs. Banks helped out at the nursery school where Joey's baby sister went; mine was a teacher's aide at the high school where my sister went.

Not that Sissy was too happy to have Mama there. She took up sassing shortly after we moved, and was all the time saying how mortifying it was to be under Mama's microscope. "I feel like a ladybug with my wings pinned flat," she'd tell her.

Mama'd just smile, then plant a kiss on the back of Sissy's curly head and say, "All bugs should be so lucky, Jenna Mae."

Sissy's sass came straight from next door, if you ask me. Straight from the mouth of Amanda Jane, who was Joey's older sister.

Amanda Jane was the same age as Sissy, and there wasn't a whole lot of difference between the two. Every bone in Jenna Mae's body was one hundred percent annoyable, just the same as Amanda Jane's.

The one place Sissy'd cut some slack was with her name. You could call her Jenna Mae, or Jenna, or Jenny, or Sissy. Didn't seem to matter to her.

But Amanda Jane? Boy! She'd fuss about every little thing *and* her name. You had to call her A-man-da-Jane, or she'd bite your head clean off.

The two of them would hang together for hours, fixing their hair and nails and smearing on makeup, gossiping about kids at the high school. Joey and me'd put our ears to the wall when we were bored, but we'd end up even more bored and quit. Girls think the dumbest things are worth wasting time over.

But all of that just gave Joey and me more reason to be friends. To escape them, we'd go exploring places I would never have gone alone—across the river, back along deer paths, or even just into town. Didn't really matter, 'cause Joey turned everything into an adventure. Shoot, that boy knew how to have more fun with *mud* than most folks have with store-bought stuff. Like one time during a frog-stranglin' rain while the rest of the world was huddling indoors, Joey took me sliding down the riverbank on trash can lids. He broke the lid handles clean off, and we went *flying*. It was the wildest time ever, and we stayed out until we were soaked to the bone and covered in mud.

Mama had a lot to say about me trackin' in mud—even though I'd stripped down best I could before coming in the house. And of course Amanda Jane and Sissy turned up their noses and told me I was dumber'n a post. Didn't spoil my mood, though. Sissy and Amanda Jane were always turning up their noses. It was something I was used to.

Or so I thought! Come baseball season, I discovered I was not immune. Sissy and Amanda Jane made Diamond Dolls, and that was the end. They thought they were the hottest things to hit Lost River since summer. They dressed up in little uniforms, wearing concession stand trays around their necks at the games. Shoot, all they were doing was selling peanuts and popcorn and Cokes, but from the way they strutted around the bleachers and around the diamond between innings you could tell they thought they were Miss America, or something.

Mrs. Banks was mighty proud of Amanda Jane, but Mama took it more in stride. "You do look cute, Jenna Mae, but I'd sure like to see you *play* something instead."

"I don't need muscles like a mountain man, Mama. It's not at*trac*tive."

Mama'd give Sissy a kiss on the cheek, Dad would tell her she was getting too big for her britches, and I'd just lay low, wondering what *was* attractive about that goofy striped hat and those matching shoes Diamond Dolls had to wear. Uglier than a bucket of armpits is what they were.

Then Mama decided we ought to go watch games, just to be supportive. Of what, I never really figured out. But we'd go and watch the ball game, without even caring who was playing against Sissy's school. We'd just swelter in the sun while Mama'd wave money in the air and buy popcorn. Ten bags she'd go through in a game, with Cokes to match, giving it away to everyone who'd take it. She'd always flag down Sissy, too. Sissy couldn't exactly *ignore* her, but she'd hand over the order, huffing and sighing like it was the world's biggest bother, and then not even say "Thank you, ma'am" like Diamond Dolls are required.

And on the drive home, Mama would always be real complimentary about the popcorn and how it was salted just right, and how the Cokes were still full of bubbles—not flat the way some Diamond Dolls let theirs get. Dad would frown at Sissy in the backseat staring out one window, and then at Amanda Jane staring out the other. And he'd say, "You girls should be more grateful to your mamas for the support you get."

Sissy would keep right on starin' out the window, and Amanda Jane would snap, "Why, my mama ain't even here!" while I'd cringe between the two of them, feeling nailed to a fence post.

Then Mama'd pat Dad's knee and say, "Well!" and start up with some other happy topic like the weather.

After we'd been to a bunch of boring games, I asked Mama, "Can Joey come?" and right off she said, "Sure. Why not." So him and A-man-da-Jane piled into the car with the rest of us, and off we went to the ballfield.

Only the whole way over Amanda Jane and Sissy were

complete cats to us. We didn't like being stuck in the middle any more'n they liked us being there, but they hissed and snarled and jabbed our ankles with their Diamond Doll sneakers—real sly, so no one in the front seat could tell what was going on.

I couldn't exactly tattle, 'cause Joey was right there putting up with it like it was nothing, but by the time we parked I was spitting mad.

"I *hate* them Diamond Dogs!" I whispered to Joey on the walk over.

"Easy, brother," he whispered back. "Them that lives by the nettle, dies by it, too."

"Huh?"

"We'll get 'em back."

"How?"

"Don't know yet, Rusty-boy, but we'll figure something."

That something happened in the third inning. Mama'd flagged Sissy down about six times already and was starting to give away popcorn and Cokes when Joey snapped his fingers and whispered, "I *got* it."

"What?"

He cocked his head. "Let's go."

So I told Mama and Dad we'd be walking around for a bit, then followed Joey out of the bleachers and around back behind the scorekeepers' tower. "Whatcha cooked up?" I asked him.

"Simple," he whispered. "You been watchin' 'em, right?"

"Who?"

"Them Diamond Dolls!"

"Uh, sorta . . ."

"Well, look. They carry all that stuff around their necks, right?"

"Sure . . ."

"Have you noticed how they carry their *own* drinks, too?"

"What do you mean?"

"To keep from dehydratin' in the sun! They got their own cup they keep sipping from right on the tray with the others."

"They drink from the same one every time?"

"Rusty-boy, come on! They're not gonna go and get lipstick on someone else's cup. They'd get fired!"

"Yeah, right, of course."

"So here's the plan—we'll catch us a couple of beetles or something, and when Jenna Mae and Amanda Jane take a break—"

"When's that gonna be?"

"How should I know? They gotta pee sometime, don't they?"

"Yeah, but—"

"And they can't lug those things into the rest rooms with 'em, right?"

"Right, but—"

"So we'll just wait until they take a break, then slip a bug or two into their Cokes."

"But—"

"Trust me, Rusty! It'll work great. They'll be drinking along, getting down to ice, and then they'll see 'em— black and crawly and dead, or maybe still creepin' around! Then they'll freak and probably send all the Cokes and popcorn flyin'. It'll be spectacular!"

My head wasn't too keen on the idea, but my ankles were all for it. So we started hunting for bugs, turning over rocks and checking under trash bins. And boy! We found some great ones. So many that we started trading up, ditching little ones for bigger ones.

Joey decided he'd get a napkin to keep them all tied up in, and pretty soon the napkin was plumped way out with bugs. So I asked him, "Why so many, Joey? We only really need two, right?"

"Yeah, but . . . I figure more'n one per cup is good insurance. What if they swallow one whole and never even know it's there? That'd be a whole lot of bother for nothing."

I looked in the napkin, thinking there were only about two you could swallow down whole, but I didn't say anything. I just nodded.

Then Joey grabbed my shoulder and said, "Quick, back here!"

So we hid around the tower and watched as Sissy and Amanda Jane peeled off their trays and put them on the ground by the side of the concession booth. And when they headed for the rest rooms, Joey snorted and said,

15

"Lucky for us those two do every little thing together. You stand guard, I'll plant the bugs. Let's go!"

So we raced over, and I stood facing out, making the best body screen I could while Joey planted the bugs. And when we heard a rest room door start to squeak open, we streaked off quicker than cats from a hose.

"Is it gonna work?" I asked when we were safe.

"I don't know! They were clingin' to the ice. They wouldn't go *down*."

"But Coke'll kill 'em, won't it? I heard it kills about anything. Then they'll drop, right?"

"They'd better!"

We hurried back to where Mama and Dad were sitting, then smiled at them real big and asked, "What's the score?"

"Score?" Mama asked me, then turned to Dad. "Jimmy? You know the score?"

"Eight–zip."

"We're losing?" Mama asked.

"We always lose, Deb." He turned to her and shook his head. "Can you explain to me again why we come to these games?"

"To be sup*p*ortive," Mama told him, then whispered, "and to help Jenna through this phase she's goin' through." She looked high and low a minute, then flagged a bill in the air at Sissy, who was coming up the steps.

Sissy rolled her eyes but came over. Only this time she actually *said* something. "Daddy," she whined, "how much Coke you gonna let her drink? Ain't you worried she'll drown?"

"Watch your tongue, Jenna Mae," he told her. "And while you're watchin' it, make it two."

"You want another one, too?"

"Yes, ma'am," he said with a frown. Then he looked at me. "How about you and Joey?"

Now I was about to say, "Sure," 'cause all that bug huntin' had worked up a wicked thirst. But then I noticed Joey's eyes, big as baseballs, his head shaking in his collar like a rattler's tail. So I said, "Uh, no sir. No, thank you."

And while Sissy's handing the Cokes over to Mama and Dad, Joey's face is all frantic, trying to tell me something.

"What?" I whispered.

He just kept on twitching at the face.

"*What?*" I asked again, only then it clicked. He hadn't put bugs in just Sissy and Amanda Jane's drinks. He'd put them in *all* the cups on their trays.

My eyes shot back and forth. From my parents to my sister. From my parents to my sister. And when I was sure no one was looking, I mouthed, "Bugs?"

He nodded.

When Sissy took off, I whispered, "*Why?*"

"Didn't want 'em to go to waste!"

I turned to Mama. She was sipping from her Coke. So was Dad. I whipped back around to Joey. "What are we gonna *do*?"

He shrugged and gave me a loopy grin. "They're not *poison* . . ."

My heart was beating double time. I watched Mama take a sip. Then another. And another. Dad, too.

I tried looking in the cup. Nothing on top. I thought about swatting at a phony gnat and knocking the cup out of Mama's hand. Thought about standing up and falling over, creatin' some sort of diversion or something.

But before I could figure out what to do, Dad spit into his hand and said, "There's a confounded *bug* in my drink!"

Mama said, "Oh, Jimmy. A little bug never hurt anything," but then she saw the shell and soggy legs and said, "Eeeew."

Dad leaned forward and poured the Coke out between the bleacher slats, real slow and steady. And when he was down to just ice he showed Mama the cup. "I told you she didn't want us here."

I looked, too. Two more bugs.

"Jenna wouldn't do such a thing . . . !" Mama said.

He took her Coke and drained it off between the slats, then handed it to her without a word.

"Oh!" Mama said, staring at the bugs in her cup. "Why . . . I can't *imagine*—"

Dad stood up and handed Mama the car keys. "You can stay if you want. I'm walking home."

"But, Jimmy—"

"I've had it with her, Deb, and I'm afraid of what I might say if I see her again before I cool off."

Mama let the keys drop in her hands and watched Dad storm down the bleachers and out of the park. And she did a lot of blinking at the bugs in her cup but didn't utter one word.

Finally, she got up and said, "I think we should be getting home, Russell."

"Uh . . . Joey and me'll just walk."

"You sure?" she asked, real distracted.

"Uh-huh. We want to watch the game."

"All right, then. If you're sure."

19

The minute she was gone, we took off on foot. And we were almost out of the park when the screaming started. Folks in the bleachers were freaking out and spilling stuff everywhere, and Sissy and Amanda Jane were running around all over the place.

I don't know how many folks actually swallowed bugs, and how many only *found* them, but I do know that that was the last day Sissy and Amanda Jane got to be Diamond Dolls. They got fired on the spot, 'cause according to their adviser, the condition of their Cokes was inexcusable.

'Course Sissy and Amanda Jane both accused *us* of being behind the bugs and hated us extra hard after that, but we swore up and down that we hadn't done it, and there wasn't a thing they could do to prove it.

Except maybe get one of us to fess up, but that was hopeless. Joey and me'd made a pact on the walk home.

Another secret, sealed for life.

3

SWAPPIN' TO AVOID A SWITCHIN'

So my family and Joey's were alike in a lot of ways. But looking back on it, it seems we were similar in ways that didn't matter, and different in ways that did.

Not different like Joey having a baby sister while I didn't. Different deeper down than that. Though Joey's little sister *was* something else.

Joey said Rhonda was like a booger that you couldn't flick off, but I thought she was cute. Shoot, her being a girl with only one name was enough right there to make me like her. But it was more the way she was always so happy to see me that I liked. She'd squeal, "Russy!" any time I'd walk through the door, then patter over and jump up and down. "Horsey! Horsey!"

So I'd give her horsey rides all over the house, kickin' and neighin' and acting like a crazy wild mustang. And of course Amanda Jane would turn her nose up and head for *our* house, but Mrs. Banks didn't seem to mind the racket, and Mr. Banks just turned up the TV and drowned us out.

Then one day after giving Rhonda the best mustang ride ever, I collapsed on my belly and said to Joey's mama,

"Ma'am, you really got to get this girl a pony." Rhonda was bouncing on me, kicking my ribs. "I can't take it no more."

"A pony? Shoot," Joey's mama said. "We can't even keep goldfish from dying. How we gonna keep a horse?"

"Horsey, horsey!" Rhonda swung off me and started tugging on her mama's sleeve. "I want a horsey!"

Mrs. Banks rolled her eyes, then stopped and said, "But that reminds me—Joey? Clean out the fishbowl, would you?"

"But, Mama! It's Rhonda's fish, not mine!"

"Joey, you help around this house, just like everyone else."

"But I just cleaned it!"

"Don't sass your mama!" Mr. Banks yelled from over by the TV.

"But I *just* did it. Yesterday!"

Joey's dad slammed down his beer and was out of his easy chair in a flash, heading straight for Joey. "Then why do them fish keep on dyin'?"

"It ain't my fault!" Joey said.

"It ain't my fault, *sir*," his dad corrected him.

Joey was backing away. "It ain't my fault, *sir*."

"Then whose fault is it? The fish?"

"Well . . . yes. Yes, sir."

Mr. Banks scowled at him. "*Yes*, sir?" He sucked in air, and his belly seemed to lift right into his chest. "Don't you make me open a can of whup-ass on you, boy. You go clean that bowl, and make it sparkle. And the next time a fish dies around here, I'm holdin' you responsible. You hear me?"

"But—"

"*Do you hear me*, boy?"

Joey cowered. "Yes, sir."

"Good. 'Cause from this minute on, every fish that dies earns you a lickin'."

"But—"

Mr. Banks gave him the most shrivelin' look I'd ever seen.

"Yes, sir," Joey choked out.

Joey's mama went up to his dad and whispered, "Bobby, maybe we should talk about this some . . . ?"

"What's there to say?" he growled at her. "You want him to help out, he's helpin' out. End of discussion."

So while Joey's dad went back to his easy chair and Joey's mama took Rhonda into the kitchen, Joey and me shuffled down to the bathroom to clean the fishbowl.

"I ain't heard him mad like *that* before," I whispered when we were out of earshot.

Joey snickered. "That was nothin'."

Now, it's funny. You go through life thinking people are pretty much alike. That the folks on your left are pretty much like the folks on your right, and that they're all pretty much the same as you. And you reckon that what goes on inside your house is pretty much what's going on inside every house on the street.

But hearing Joey's dad yell like that made the whole inside of Joey's house feel different. Strange. And I could tell it made Joey feel strange, too, but I couldn't tell if that was because I was there to hear it or if it would've felt strange to him regardless. So I tried to ease the strain a little by saying, "My dad gets pretty fried at me sometimes, too."

"Yeah?" he said, and he sounded hopeful.

"*Real* fried," I said, trying to remember the last time Dad had yelled at me.

"Does he make you get your own switch?"

"Yeah," I lied.

"Hurts like hell."

"No kiddin'."

The bathroom light was already on, and there were little blue streaks of toothpaste smeared all over the counter. "That stupid Rhonda," Joey said, taking a worn washcloth to the toothpaste. "I catch it for this all the time, too."

"Just tell him it's Rhonda's."

"He don't care."

"Well, try tellin' him when he ain't heated."

"It'll just *get* him heated."

Then I noticed the goldfish bowl. "Uh-oh."

"What?" he said, wiping down the sink.

I closed the door tight.

"What you doin'?"

I pointed to the fish, floating on top. "It's already dead."

"It *can't* be." Joey hung his face over the bowl. "Maaaaan!"

"Just *tell* him. It can't be your fault . . . you just *got* here. And look—the water's clean as can be."

Joey shook his head. "Don't matter what I tell him, he don't *listen.*"

We stared at the fish, all bug-eyed on his side.

"What're we gonna do?" I asked him.

"Flush it."

"And *then* what?"

"Shoot, I don't know. Get another?"

"How?"

Joey scratched his head. "You up for a hike?"

"I reckon we better *run.*"

So we did. Out the back door, around the blackberry bushes, behind the neighbor's yard, then down Pickett Lane and clear into town. And when we got to Wet Pets all out of breath and sweaty, Joey didn't even slow down. He just jingled through the door and headed straight for the goldfish tank, where there was a sign boasting, SALE: 25¢

"Afternoon," said the man behind the cash register, and after a minute he made his way out to us. "After a wet pet?"

There must've been a zillion goldfish in the tank, some brown, some spotted, and some pure orange. "That one," Joey said, tapping on the glass.

The man laughed. "Can't guarantee I can catch that *pa'ticular* one, but—"

"Oh, no, sir," Joey said, all wide-eyed. "It's gotta be that one."

"Which one?"

"That one right there," he said, tapping like crazy.

So the man lowered in a net and caught about six others before snagging the right one.

"That's it!" Joey said.

The man freed the fish in a baggie of water and tied it off. "Need food? A bowl? Rocks? Maybe a little sea grass?"

"Got everything we need!" Joey said, slapping down a quarter.

We charged out of there, jostling that goldfish the whole way back. And when we slipped it in the bowl, its little brain must've been mighty scrambled 'cause it spun around like crazy for a few minutes before settling in.

Joey shook in some food and whispered, "*Live*, you stupid thing, live!"

Two days later we were charging back to Wet Pets.

"I don't *get* it," Joey said on the run home. "What am I doin' wrong?"

"Got me," I said. "I think you'd have better luck with a horse."

Rhonda noticed, all right, only she didn't understand what she was noticing. "Oh, look! Goldilocks grew an extra spot!"

"Where?" Joey said, looking in the bowl. "Where?"

"Right there! On her tail!"

"You sure?"

"Uh-huh."

Two days later, Goldi was floating on her side.

"Shoot!" Joey cried, and this time he got himself two fish—one new Goldi and one backup Goldi.

"Where you gonna keep the backup?" I asked him.

"Under the bed."

"You can't keep doin' this forever."

"*You* want to take my switchin'?"

"Just *talk* to him about it."

"Dad don't *talk*, Rusty, he switches and he yells."

"But—"

"Don't *even*," he said, stopping me. "It only makes things worse."

So I let it be. But it didn't seem fair. Not fair at all. And it bugged me that I couldn't do something about it.

So one night at supper I asked Dad, "How come Joey and me are friends, and Sissy and Amanda Jane are friends, but you and Mama don't ever do nothin' with their parents?"

"Don't ever do *anything*," Mama corrected.

Dad was just studying me from across the table, so I added, "Lots of folks get together for barbeque. Maybe sit on the porch? The river's right there, why don't you and Joey's dad ever go fishin' together?" I turned to Mama. "Or shoppin'. Lots of ladies do that."

Mama looked at her plate; Dad looked straight at me, bobbing his head a little. Finally he said, "Adults tend to get caught up in the running of their families."

"But . . . we could run our families together, or something."

He just stared at me.

"From time to time?"

"Would you like that?" Mama asked.

I shrugged. "Joey might."

"Well, *I* wouldn't," Sissy said.

Dad looked her over a minute. "Why's that, Jenna Mae?"

"He scares me."

"Joey does?" Mama asked her.

"No!" she said, looking at Mama like she was dumber than a mud fence.

"Jenna . . . ," Dad warned.

"But, Daddy, how could that little twerp possibly *scare* me?"

"Do not use that tone with us, young lady," he said.

She sighed and turned to Mama. "I was referrin' to their daddy, Mama."

Dad nodded a little.

Mama did, too.

And no one said a word after that until dessert.

4

GAGGY GOLDFISH

Joey swapped out goldfish for weeks. Every few days he got himself a backup. Every few days he flushed another Goldi down the toilet. We were becoming real regulars at the fish store, but no one ever questioned what we were doing with all those fish.

Then one day we stopped in at Wet Pets after school, and the girl behind the counter said, "You boys would be money ahead to get yourself some conditioner."

Joey pulled a face at her. "That stuff's for girls!"

She stared at him a minute, then laughed. "Not *hair* conditioner, dummy. *Water* conditioner."

Joey puffed out his chest. "Who you callin' a dummy?"

"You," she laughed. "You're Amanda Jane's little brother, ain'tcha?"

I slid a look Joey's way, thinking, Uh-oh.

"So?" he said, puffing up even bigger.

"So she told me all about you swapping out fish."

"She . . . did?"

"To avoid a switchin'?"

We both just stared at her.

"You . . . you friends with her?" Joey finally asked.

"Sure. And don't worry. I ain't gonna tattle. Neither's she."

He shook his head. "You don't know Amanda Jane."

"Sure I do. Now here. Let's get you a fish, and let's get you some conditioner." She put the net in and kept on talking. "Ain't you read your goldfish care sheet?"

"What care sheet?"

"The care sheet everybody gets when they buy their first goldfish!"

"We didn't get no care sheet!"

She scooped up a nice, healthy gold one with just the right amount of white. "Sure you did—unless you were in too hot a hurry to take one."

Joey and me looked at each other, then I said, "Well, what's the sheet say?"

She set the fish free in the baggie of water. "It says if you use tap water, which I'm guessin' you do . . ." She raised an eyebrow at Joey, and when he nodded she went on, "And you don't have aeration, which I'm guessin' you don't . . ."

"Aeration?"

"A bubbler? Do you have one of those?"

He shook his head.

"Then you need a few drops of water conditioner, and maybe a pinch of aquarium salt to keep off diseases."

"Salt?"

"Well, the salt's optional." She tied off the bag. "How much money you got?"

"Not much. How much for the conditioner?"

"Oh, five bucks or so."

"That's twenty fish worth!"

She shrugged. "You can keep runnin' back and forth your entire life, I don't care." She carried the fish over to the register, asking, "How you been cleanin' the bowl?"

"Real, real good!" Joey said.

"With soap?"

"Tons of it!"

She slapped a yellow goldfish care sheet in front of us and circled the line that said, "do NOT use soap," then pulled a small bottle of water conditioner off the shelf behind her. "Here. This one's only three bucks." She grinned. "Or twelve fish, if that's how you want to figure it." Then she added, "But as of next week, it'll only be six fish."

"Huh?" Joey said, looking up from the sheet. "How come?"

"Mr. Huber told me the sale's over on Monday. Price is goin' back up to fifty cents a fish."

Joey dug deep for cash.

On the walk home, Joey was quiet for the longest time. And when we reached the corner of Pickett and Lee, he sat right down by the side of the road, even though the light was steady green.

I stood over him. "What's wrong, Joey?"

He shook his head. "I don't get it."

"About the fish?"

"Nah, about Amanda Jane."

I sat next to him. "You mean that she didn't tattle?"

"Uh-huh. I'm dumbstruck, is what I am. Amanda Jane *hates* me."

I tried to imagine Sissy keeping a secret like that from our dad, and just couldn't. "It's a wonder," I told him. "A real wonder."

"She ain't even tried blackmailin' me."

I nodded. "Come to think of it, it's more like a miracle."

"But *why* didn't she?"

"Maybe she's savin' it up."

"Hmm." He nodded. "More'n likely."

"Or maybe she likes you better'n she likes your dad."

He turned to face me, and I buttoned my lip quick. I couldn't tell *what* was going through that boy's head, but it didn't look good.

Finally he stood up and said, "Rusty-boy, sometimes you're smarter'n I give you credit for."

No one was home at Joey's house, and the fish in the bowl was still gulpin' around. So we parked the backup Goldi under Joey's bed, then got busy cleaning the fishbowl like the yellow sheet instructed. And when we were all done, we put in some water conditioner, slipped the goldfish back in, and waited.

"Seems fine," Joey said at last.

"Better'n fine. Why don'tcha feed him?"

We read the instructions about that, too, and sprinkled in just a little.

"Looks happy," I told him when the food was mostly gone.

"We'll see," he said, and hid the conditioner and instructions under the sink.

The next morning when I picked him up on the way to school, I asked, "Well?"

"Still kickin'."

A week later it was *still* alive. Joey was in a fine mood about it, too, 'cause during class he sketched a fish with an X for an eye and a talkie bubble that said, "I'm trying to croak, but I can't!"

Joey was all the time sketching goofy things and holding them up at me when the teacher wasn't looking. Half the time they cracked me up so bad I'd get scolded, or once even thrown out of the room. How are you supposed to "Control yourself!" when someone flashes you a picture of a monkey's butt that's labeled TEACHER'S BRAIN?

Anyway, from his fish picture, I could tell he was feeling pretty confident about Goldi, so on the walk home from school, I asked, "Whatcha gonna do about the backup?"

He shrugged. "Guess I can flush it."

"Is it still in the bag?"

He nodded. "I put it in a bigger one and I've been

feeding it, just in case. But it gasps around for air, and I reckon it's about through anyway."

"Why don'tcha put it in the bowl with the other one?"

"Nah."

"Rhonda won't mind. Just tell her Goldilocks had a baby."

"It's bigger'n Goldi!" he said.

"Don't matter."

He thought about it, then said, "Nuh-uh. I'm flushin' it."

"Joey!"

"Don't be a wuss."

That shut me up, but only for a minute. "Why don'tcha just give it back to Wet Pets?"

"Look, Rusty-boy. I don't want to be caught with the thing, and I ain't walking it clear back to Wet Pets. I'm flushin' it."

Joey's dad's truck was in the drive, so we slipped in the back way to do the deed. I thought it'd be better to go in front like everything was normal, but Joey was all obsessed with flushing the fish before anyone knew we were even around. So we snuck the backup into the bathroom and shut the door.

Now I told Joey to dump the water *and* the fish together, but he said he didn't want to. "I always drain it first," he told me.

"Why?"

"Just hush up, would you?"

So I watched him open the bag and drain the water into the sink, then clamp a hand over the fish as it was flopping around. But just when he was moving for the toilet, the door burst open and his dad came barging in.

Mr. Banks jumped back, and so did we. But he recovered first, growling, "Where'd the two of you come from?"

"School . . . ," Joey said, backing away.

"What you got there, boy?" I was between the two of them, so he shoved me aside, saying, "Out of my way, Cooper!" then moved in on Joey, who was hunched over with his back to us. "Stand up!" Mr. Banks said, yanking Joey up by his shirt and spinning him around.

Joey's face looked watery and red.

"What are you two up to in here?" his dad yelled.

"Feedin' the fish!" Joey said. "We's just feedin' the fish!"

Joey's dad looked at him, all ruddy-faced and squinty-eyed. "Let's see your hands, boy."

Joey put out his hands.

They were empty.

His dad kept right on squinting and said, "Spread yourself."

So Joey turned to face the wall, then planted his hands above the towel rack and his feet apart. His dad frisked him over good, then turned to me. "You, too."

It felt hot as the hinges of hell in that bathroom. But there was no escapin', so I did like Joey'd done and put my hands on the wall. Joey's dad kicked my feet apart, the smell of beer sweating from his pores as he frisked me over twice.

When he was done, he spun me by the shoulder and said, "I'm beginnin' to think you're a bad influence on my son, Cooper."

I swallowed hard and said, "Yes, sir," 'cause it felt like no other answer would get me out alive.

"Get! Both of you, get!" he hollered, pointing at the door. Then he grumbled, "What a man's got to go through to use his own john" and slammed it shut behind us.

The minute we were safe outside, I whispered, "Where's the fish?"

Joey pointed to his stomach.

My eyes bugged out. "You didn't!"

He nodded. "And it's still alive."

"What? Can't be!"

"I swallowed it whole."

"No!"

"I wasn't gonna take time to *chew*." He pulled a face and dragged me along. "Man, it's floppin' around in there!"

"Where we goin'?"

"To your house."

"What are we gonna do there?"

He held his stomach. "Oh, man! I gotta get this thing outta me!"

We went straight to the bathroom and locked ourselves in. Joey flung up the toilet seat, got on his knees, and stuck his finger clear down his throat. And he gagged and choked and gave sort of a half heave, but no fish came up.

"I need something longer." He looked over his shoulder. "Hand me your toothbrush!"

"My *tooth*brush?"

"Hurry! It's floppin' around!"

I gave him Sissy's toothbrush instead.

It worked like a charm, 'cause thirty seconds later that fish came flying out his throat and landed in the bowl.

Joey recovered and wiped his face, then we watched Goldi's backup floating on its side in the middle of chunks of food and acid.

"It's *dead*?" Joey said. He poked it a bunch with the end of Sissy's toothbrush. "*Now* it decides to go and die?"

We stared at it another minute. Then Joey gave me a loopy grin and flushed it down the toilet.

5

PLINKING

I never actually saw a gun before I met Joey Banks. Not up close, anyway. But it turned out Joey *owned* one. His very own .22 rifle. Got it for his twelfth birthday.

The first time I saw him with it, it scared me a little, 'cause Dad had always told me to turn tail and *run* should any of my friends be brandishing weapons. But Joey wasn't exactly brandishing. He was sitting cross-legged on the ground, plinking at cans set up in front of the Bankses' big ol' blackberry patch.

Joey must've seen my face, 'cause he said, "You never shot a gun before?" and when I shook my head, he said, "Shoot, there ain't nothin' dangerous about it. You just need to treat it with respect." So I didn't turn tail and run. I stood behind him and watched.

After a few more shots he said, "Come *on*, Rusty-boy. It ain't gonna bite."

So I moved a few steps closer to where he was sitting.

"Right *here*," he said, patting the ground beside him. "Watch and learn."

I just stayed put, but after he'd knocked over all his

cans, he lay the gun down next to him and said, "Help me set 'em up again, would you?" And while we put the cans back up, he said, "Whatcha worried about? It's just good clean fun." I didn't say anything, so he tried again. "Look here. If I miss a shot—even if one goes completely *wild*—ain't nothin' gonna get hurt."

I watched him plink down all the cans again, and dust the ground a few times besides. "See?" he said when the gun was empty. "Safer'n watchin' TV."

I laughed. "Nothin's safer'n watchin' TV, Joey."

"Oh, I don't know 'bout *that*," he said, casting a look over his shoulder. But before I could ask what he meant, he said, "Are you gonna try this, or what?"

"I don't know . . . ," I told him.

"Shoot, come here. I'll give you an official lesson."

So we set up the cans again, then sat in the dirt with the rifle across both our laps. "Geez, quit shakin', Rusty-boy. You're actin' like a wuss."

"Sorry," I told him.

"It's a *tool*, is all. Like a shovel or a car. Won't hurt nothin' unless you point it in the wrong direction."

I nodded.

"Okay, then. This here's the muzzle. You never want to point it at anybody, even if the gun's not loaded. This here's the stock. You know that much, right?"

I nodded.

"The ammo goes in here . . ." He started feeding .22s into the side of the gun. "This rifle'll take about ten rounds." When he had it loaded, he said, "The empty shells pop out here when you cock the lever forward." He put all four fingers in the lever and pushed forward, then pulled back.

"But nothin' came out," I told him.

"That's 'cause we ain't shot off a round yet. But now we got a round in the chamber." He looked at me. "See how the hammer's pulled back like that?"

I nodded.

"Means it's ready to fire." He laughed. "Assumin' you put your rounds in right, that is."

I wasn't ready to laugh about anything yet, so I just waited.

"At *this* point you don't want to be waggin' this thing around," he said, wagging the thing around. "At *this* point you could kill something, so keep your finger off the trigger. Got that? No touchin' the trigger 'til you're ready to shoot."

I swallowed and nodded.

He went on with his lesson. "Now, knowing how to aim makes the difference between knowing how to shoot and just messin' around." His face moved in close to mine, and he whispered, "You ready for the secret?"

"There's a secret?" I whispered back.

"Uh-huh," he said, then pointed to a little bead at the front of the barrel. "And this here is it."

"That there's the secret?"

"Uh-huh. The secret to actually hittin' something."

I looked at it closer. It was just a little black bead of metal. Barely even there. So I sat back again and said, "Quit messin' with me, Joey."

"I ain't messin' with you, Russ! I'm dead serious. I'm a sharpshooter, and the reason's simple: I pay attention to my front sight."

"That's what that speck is? Your front sight?"

"Uh-huh. And here's the secret," he said all excited-like, then started drawing in the dirt. "What you want to do is take your front sight and line it up like so. So it's smack-dab in the middle of the little saddle of your back sight."

"Where's the back sight?"

He pointed to a little nick in the middle of a half-inch piece of metal on the back part of the barrel.

41

"That don't look like much."

"But the two of them together's everything." He held the gun up for me. "Here, have a look."

So I pinched one eye closed and looked down the top of the barrel, trying to line up the speck and the nick, just like he'd drawn in the dirt.

"Got it?"

"Uh, yeah. I think so."

"Look at the *front* sight, Rusty. Not the close one. That's what you focus on—the front sight."

"You don't look at the can?"

"Should be nothin' but a blur when you press the trigger."

"I didn't know that."

"Well remember it, 'cause that's the secret." He took the gun back and wedged it against his shoulder. "Okay now. This is how you hold it. Nice and firm. Only kicks a little, but still, hold it nice and firm. Then find yourself a can, line up your sights, focus on the front one, and"—he pulled the trigger back—"press."

The gun fired and jerked back a little, and the first can tumbled. Then he cocked the lever out and back, ejecting the empty shell into the dirt. He smiled at me. "You ready to give it a shot?"

I was over being scared. So I nodded and said, "Yeah, I think so."

"Attaboy, Rusty! Aim for the stew can. It's biggest."

The gun was heavier than it looked, and at first the tip of it wobbled around something fierce. I kept losing track of the can, then the sight, then the can . . . But finally I pulled the trigger—which was actually *easier* than I thought it'd be—and felt the butt jerk against my shoulder.

"Nice try, Rusty," he said.

The can was still standing tall.

"Shoot!"

"Hey, it was your first shot," he said. "At least it went downrange. Try again."

So I cocked the lever out and back. It felt firm and strong. Powerful. I raised the gun, lined the sights, pulled the trigger, then looked.

One stew can, still standing tall.

"Shoot!"

"You was closer that time," he told me. "It dusted right in front. Try again."

I cocked the hand lever back with more confidence this time, raised the gun, and pulled the trigger.

"Shoot!"

"Don't jerk the trigger, Rusty. Squeeze it nice and easy. A little jerk on this end sends the barrel way off target."

I pushed the lever out and back, fast and steady. "All right, y'stupid can . . . ," I muttered, then lined up the sights and pulled the trigger back, nice and easy.

Plink!

"Ya did it! Rusty-boy, ya did it!"

Snap-clack! I cocked the next round in. Nice and steady . . . *Plink!* I grinned and did it again. And again. And pretty soon the gun was empty and I was reloading and plinking down the next round of cans.

"You're *good*," Joey told me when we'd run out of ammo.

"It's *fun*," I said.

"See? Nothin' to be scared of. Nothin' at all."

That night at supper when Dad asked what was new with everyone, I didn't volunteer about my plinkin' session with Joey. I just let Mama chatter on about the high school and how the copying machine had jammed and printed a bunch of tests upside down and backward, and how she had to do them all over twice.

"Tests?" Sissy asked, tuning in. "What tests?"

Mama raised an eyebrow at her. "None of your business what tests, Jenna."

"It's the sophomore Civil War exam, ain't it?"

"*Isn't* it," Mama corrected, then gave her a wicked grin. "And I ain't tellin'."

"Mama!"

Mama laughed. "Jenna Mae, I can't tell you that. It'd be totally against the rules, not to mention my morals."

"Just *tellin'* me's against your *morals?*"

Mama nodded. "'Cause the next thing you're gonna want to know is if there's questions on what month the South seceded, and who the provisional president of the Confederacy was, and what date Sherman stormed Fort McAllister, and . . ."

"We gotta know all *that?*"

"I'm not sayin' you do, and I'm not sayin' you don't. But I can tell you this—it's a twenty-two-page test, and you better start studying a lot harder than you been."

"Twenty-two pages!"

"I'm sure Mr. Hickle's told you that."

"Just that it's multiple choice. Not that it's twenty-two pages!"

"He's told you to study, though, right?"

"Well, sure, but the test ain't for another few weeks!"

Mama shot her a look over a fork loaded with peas. "*Isn't* for another few weeks, but I'm telling you—you better start studying *now.*"

Everyone was quiet a minute, then Dad said, "I think

you should thank your mama for the warnin', Jenna Mae."

"Thank you for the warnin', Mama," Jenna Mae said dutifully, but she was scowling, boy. Scowling but good.

"So," Dad said, turning to me. "How about you, son?"

"How about me?"

"Anything new to report?"

"Nah," I told him, but after a minute I felt a confession was in order. "Uh, the truth is, there is something."

He buttered a biscuit. "And what's that?"

"Joey taught me how to shoot his twenty-two rifle today."

Dad's butter knife came slidin' to a halt.

"It was like a lesson, Dad. Very professional."

"Joey? Professional?" he asked, his face all contorted.

"Yes, sir. He taught me the parts of the gun, taught me about safety, and he taught me about how to actually *hit* something. I'm good, Dad! I'm real good. And it was fun!"

Mama's jaw was danglin'. Sissy looked like she'd bit her own tail, and Dad seemed frozen in place.

Mama choked out, "They've got *guns* over there?"

"I don't know about *guns*, Mama. Joey's got a twenty-two, is all. Got it when he turned twelve. It's just a tool, same as a shovel or a car—you just don't want to turn it in the wrong direction."

"Is that so?" Dad asked me.

"Yes, sir! And at first I was gonna race right home like you told me I should if someone was messin' with a gun, but Joey wasn't *messin'*. He was sharpshootin'. And it was safe! I swear to howdy, it was totally safe!"

Sissy made the sourest face ever and said, "I hope you ground him good, Daddy."

Dad cocked his head at her. "For tellin' us the truth, Jenna Mae?"

"For playin' with a gun!"

"Hmmm," he said, then pushed back from the table.

"Where you going, Jimmy?" Mama called after him.

Dad came back with a gun in his hands.

"What?" Sissy gasped. "We got one of them in *our* house?"

"Oh, Jimmy," Mama said. "You think this is a good idea?"

"I want to see the boy's safety tips."

"Here?" Mama asked. "At the supper table?"

He nodded and handed the gun over.

So I gave him a tour of what I'd learned, and repeated all the rules Joey'd taught me. And when I was all done, Dad nodded a little and said, "Well. It seems Joey's done a fine job teachin' you, son. There's only one thing I might add."

"What's that, sir?"

He looked me right in the eye. "Guns are not toys. Don't point them at something you're not willing to destroy, and always, *always* treat them like they're loaded whether you think they are or not."

I nodded.

"Repeat after me, Russell: All guns are always loaded."

"All guns are always loaded."

"Are we clear on that?"

"Yes, sir."

"All right then. Tomorrow I want to see where you and Joey have been plinkin'. I want to see your safety rules in action, and then if it all checks out, you have my permission."

"To go plinkin'?"

He nodded. "You're old enough, son. As long as you're safe, and as long as you tell me about it if you ever see Joey *not* being safe."

"Yes, sir!"

"All right then."

Mama whispered, "Are you sure about this, Jimmy?" but Dad just nodded.

"I don't *believe* this," Sissy whined. "He went and shot a gun and you ain't gonna ground him?"

"Eat your supper," Dad told her, then heaped some more butter on his biscuit.

6

SAY "AAAAH . . ."

Joey's dad did have a soft spot. It was for their mouser Smoky. "This cat works harder than the whole brood combined," he'd announce anytime Smoky'd lay a mouse at his feet.

Mrs. Banks would watch him toss the mouse in the kitchen trash and say, "You expectin' Rhonda to sweep the drive and trim the thickets back?"

"No," he'd grumble, grabbing a beer from the fridge. "But it'd be nice if *some*one around here would." Then he'd flop in his easy chair, put Smoky up on his lap, and watch TV.

"Amen to that," Joey's mama would mutter, then get back to cleaning floors.

Now, there ain't no way Amanda Jane was gonna sweep the drive or trim back blackberries. She was like Sissy—fearful that muscles might start bulging out should she lift a finger. So that left Joey for the yard chores and the shuttlin' of trash and such.

Then one Saturday shortly after Joey and me'd given Dad a righteous demonstration of gun safety and marksmanship, I went over to the Bankses' and found Joey sweating it out on his driveway, sweeping off dirt.

"Hey, Rusty," he said. "Come to help?"

I'd just skinned by having to yank weeds from Mama's flower beds, so sweepin' the Bankses' drive wasn't exactly what I had in mind. "Think maybe we can do some plinkin' later on?"

"Maybe after I finish the drive." He pushed his broom along real slow, grating sand across asphalt.

"How long do you suppose that'll be?"

He stopped and hung on the handle, then looked at the sun creepin' its way to high noon. "Hotter it gets, the slower I move." He shoved the broom forward a few strokes. "Same as most creatures on this miserable earth."

"Miserable earth? Geez, Joey. What's eatin' you?"

"What's eatin' me?" *Swish . . . swish.* "I'll tell you what's eatin' me. Right now the TV's on inside. It's still cool in there, and Dad's sittin' back with his feet propped high. Mama's workin', but Amanda Jane's fixin' her face, and Rhonda is probably makin' a mess somewhere that'll get me whupped." He pushed sand off the edge of the drive. "And with the way these godforsaken ground squirrels keep kickin' up dirt, this here's like rakin' rain."

It was true. There were holes and mounds all along the Bankses' drive. "Have you tried drownin' them out?" I asked him. "I heard squirrels hate water."

"Don't work."

"How about Coke? I heard they can't take the bubbles. That they explode or somethin'."

"Don't work. Goes flat before they drink it."

"Bubble gum?"

"No, Rusty-boy. That don't work either." Then he noticed something. He moved closer to his dad's truck, saying, "Well, will you look at that . . ."

"What?" I looked under the fender, too.

"There! The wheel's sunk right in."

Now the Bankses' drive wasn't in the greatest shape to begin with. The oil coat was mostly gone, and little rocks were showing through everywhere—which did make sweeping it a great big job.

But there weren't any *holes* in it. At least none before that one.

"They're diggin' *under* the drive, those varmints!"

"Think so?"

"What *else* could be causin' that? I'll bet if I . . ." He jammed his foot alongside the truck, near where the tire was sunk in, and made a deep dent. "Look at that!"

Just then Joey's dad came out the front door, calling, "What y'all think you're doin' by my truck?"

"Come look at this!" Joey called back.

"What?" he said, stepping off the porch.

"Them stupid squirrels is burrowin' under the drive! Your tire's sunk clear in!"

I don't think Joey's dad believed him at first, but when he saw the hole he let out some mighty hot language.

And when he was all done blowin' his top over that, he turned to Joey and said, "I'm tired of messin' around with them things. I'll give you a buck a tail for 'em."

"A buck a tail? You mean shoot 'em with my twenty-two?"

"Yeah. Enough plinkin'. Time you did something real with that gun."

"But a buck a tail?" Joey was grinning from ear to ear.

"Listen, boy. I ain't givin' you no buck for *sayin'* you got one. I want you to do like Smoky and bring it to me. No body, no buck."

"Yes, sir!" Joey said, all excited.

Joey's dad turned his back on us and headed for the house. And when he got on the porch he yelled, "Don't just stand there, boy! Get your gun!"

We set up in the shade of the eaves with the .22, a box of shells, and two tall glasses of sweet tea.

Beat sweeping the drive, that's for sure.

But after we'd sat there maybe half an hour with no action, I whispered, "Maybe we need some bait? Like peanuts or somethin'?"

"Great idea, Rusty-boy!" Joey said, springing to his feet. "I'll be back in a flash."

Now, while he was gone, I saw something out of the corner of my eye. Something across the drive. It was just a little flash of gray, but when I focused in on it, I thought it might be a ground squirrel, peeking up from its hole.

I picked up the gun and waited.

Yup, that's what it was, inching forward, twitching its way out of the hole.

Very slowly, I lifted the gun to my shoulder.

Lined up the sights.

And when the squirrel was full-on out of its hole, standing on its hind legs, twitching its nose at the air, I squeezed the trigger.

It screeched, then flopped over three times and just lay there.

Right after, my *stomach* screeched, then flopped over three times and about came up my throat.

"Rusty, you got one! You got one!" Joey cried, jumping off the porch. He charged across the driveway, found the squirrel, then picked it up by the tail, cryin', "Way to go!"

Maybe it's me that's dumber than a mud fence, but when I'd picked up the gun, I hadn't actually pictured *killing* something. Right then, that squirrel was just a moving target. One step up from plinkin' at cans.

But when it screeched . . . boy, that was like a slug in the gut. Cans don't screech. They just fall over. But the squirrel . . . I'd *hurt* the squirrel. Shoot, I'd *killed* the squirrel.

It took that screech to teach me—squirrels ain't stew cans.

"Rusty! You done good!" Joey cried, and hauled the squirrel over to me. "Look at this thing! Deader than a doornail!"

I lay the gun down and looked away.

"Rust? Boy, you look kinda green."

"I killed it, Joey," I choked out.

"Amen to that!" he said, then sat down beside me. "Look. You don't feel bad for squishin' bugs, right? Ants, spiders, flies, mosquitoes . . . none of them makes you squeamy, right?"

I shrugged. "Those're bugs."

He held the squirrel up. "This here's just an oversized bug, only he's too big to squish with your shoe." He pointed across the drive. "They're just oversized termites, borin' holes everywhere. First the hillside, then the drive . . . pretty soon the whole *house* is gonna collapse, all 'cause these critters can't keep to themselves."

"I don't know, Joey . . ."

"Look," he said, tossing the squirrel aside. "It just takes some gettin' used to, is all."

"How come you're used to it already?"

He shrugged and picked up the gun. "I hate them things." He scowled. "If you'd been sweepin' my drive for years, you'd hate 'em, too."

I wanted to get up and go, but I was still workin' back my stomach. Last thing I wanted was to puke in front of Joey. It'd be so wuss-like.

So I waited for my stomach to settle a bit, but then I went and riled it up all over again by glancing at that fuzzy gray carcass. Its eyes were wide open. Its paws were hanging. Like any minute it might spring up and run off. I couldn't even see any blood.

Joey squatted back against the house with the gun

propped on his knee. "Dad says I don't need no peanuts. Says whistlin' brings 'em up."

"Whistlin' does?"

"Uh-huh. Said to do it like this," and he gave a little whistle. One note, kinda low and sharp.

We waited, and finally I whispered, "I don't see nothin'."

He whistled again.

Nothing.

"Maybe they're scared off from the one I got."

"They's dumb, Rusty. Dumber'n anything." He whistled again.

My stomach was settled enough for me to get up and go, which is what I was fixin' to do, only just then Joey whispered, "There!"

Another gray face was twitching out of its hole.

Rusty whistled again.

The squirrel came up further, twitching its nose from side to side.

Joey raised the gun and pinched an eye closed. "C'mon, ya varmint!" He whistled again, and the minute the squirrel came out of the hole, *pop!* The gun fired.

I had pinched *both* my eyes closed, but they shot open when I heard Joey cuss. "What happened?" I asked him.

"Didn't you see that? He somersaulted and ran off. How could he run off? Shoot! I ain't never gonna find him in them blackberry bushes!"

"You sure you hit him?"

"Yeah! Smack in the shoulder. He's probably gone off to die back there. Dang!"

I stood up and said, "Well, I'd best be goin'."

"See ya," he said, then shook his head. "Dang! How could he run off?"

I went home and lay on my bed for a bit, feeling bad about the squirrel. It didn't help any, so I went outside and started yanking weeds from Mama's flower beds. I kept an ear perked for the pop of the .22, wondering how many dollars Joey was up to. And I tried to tell myself that Joey was right—that ground squirrels were nothin' but vermin—but my stomach was having trouble believing it.

After a while Dad came out and said, "Son, I don't think I've ever seen you work this hard without bein' asked. Something bothering you?"

55

"Nah," I said, yanking up another weed.

He sat on the stoop of the porch. "Thought I heard plinkin' next door. Not in the mood?"

"He ain't plinkin' cans, Dad. He's killin' ground squirrels."

"Ah," he said, wrapping one knee with his hands. "Seem like cruelty to you?"

I yanked up a weed and flung it to the ground. "They're so cute!"

He nodded. "Cute and mighty destructive."

"I killed one, Dad! It *screeched*."

He was still a minute, then shrugged. "Lot less cruel than poison."

"But, Dad—"

"Don't be hard on yourself, Russell. Just don't go back over if it bothers you."

I nodded, then got back to pulling weeds. And when I had the flower beds all picked clean, I hauled the weeds around back to the trash and wandered next door. It'd been a long time since I'd heard the gun go off.

Joey was still at it, though, hunkered down under the eaves further back along the house with a stack of ground squirrels by his side.

"Man," I said when I saw his pile. "How many you got?"

"Six," he whispered.

56 For some reason six didn't seem as bad as one. I don't know why. "How long you gonna be doin' this?"

"Long as it takes."

"Don'tcha want to go do something fun?"

"This *is* fun, Rusty-boy. The funnest six bucks I've ever made. *And*," he added, "I discovered the secret."

"What's that?"

"You whisper, 'Say Aaaah!'"

"Say Aaaah?"

"Yep."

"What's that do?"

"Hit 'em in the shoulder or the butt or even the chest, they run off and die in the thicket. Hit 'em in the mouth and it's over quick."

I was getting ready to head home again when he said, "Shhh. You see that?"

"What?"

"In the bushes, right back there!"

I did see it. A little patch of gray, inching through the thicket. But I didn't want to see him kill another one, so I said, "I don't see nothin'."

"Right back there!" He raised his gun. "Probably one of those suckers I hit before that slinked away."

"I think you're seein' stuff, Joey."

"Rusty-boy, get your eyes checked. It's right back there!" He made his squirrel-call whistle, then muttered, "Come out, sucker, come on out and say Aaaah!"

I closed my eyes, wishing I'd never come back over. And when the gun popped, I thought, That's it. I'm not looking. I'm outta here.

But the sound that followed the pop wasn't a screech.

It was a high, airy, stretched-out *me-ow*.

Joey and me looked at each other with bug eyes for a solid minute. Finally, he looked over both shoulders and whispered, "Can't be."

"We gotta check, Joey."

"I'm dead, Russ. I'm dead and gone." He was sweating and panting like I'd never seen.

"You ain't dead, Joey. Come on, maybe he'll be okay. Maybe it wasn't even him!"

We inched over to the blackberry thicket and found

him right away. Smoky the Mouser was the one that was dead and gone.

Joey looked around, then stuffed him up his shirt quick and told me, "Meet me down by the river. And bring a shovel!"

I didn't even think to argue. Killing the family cat was way worse than killing the family fish. Way worse than killing a whole *school* of family fish. And knowing Joey's dad, this was something we had to hide. Quick.

So I raced home and snuck a shovel down to the water. And after we'd buried Smoky good and covered the spot with rocks, Joey and me punched knuckles and shared blood.

Another secret, sealed for life.

Then I went home and hid in my room, jumpy as spit on a skillet.

7

SQUISHIN' OUT GREEN TOMATOES

Once in a great while Mama'd say, "You're broody and bored and draggin' through chores. . . . I don't need you moodin' up the place. Go! Just go outside and be a boy."

I never knew what that meant, exactly, but I did know it set me free from her chores. I'd tear out of the house and hit the swimming hole or catch frogs, or just sit on a nice tall rock and watch the river float by.

Sometimes I went off to be a boy by myself, but most times I dragged Joey along. Not that there was any real dragging involved. If he could get away, he was more than happy to.

So one weekend, I was bored to my toes from doing stuff around the house for Mama. Every time I thought I was done, she'd stack another one on. She had me do the *dustin'*, if you can imagine that. You can't expect a boy to dust and be happy, and I told her so, but she just gave me a soothing look and said, "Won't kill ya, Russell. Besides, I love you extra for doin' it."

"Does that mean you're hatin' Sissy right now? 'Cause she ain't doing nothin'."

"She's studyin' for that big Civil War exam, and you know it. She can't advance if she flunks it, so as long as she's preparin' for that, I'm not going to call her home to dust."

I wiped the cloth across a side table. "I bet she ain't even studyin'."

"Sure she is. And if you want to go study something, you can get out of dustin', too."

"There ain't nothin' to study!"

"There isn't *anything* to study, and I'm sure there is." She looked up from her laundry folding. "You want to get out of dusting? Go write that fifty times."

"Go write what fifty times?"

"Isn't anything."

"Huh?"

"Go write 'isn't anything' fifty times."

"What *for?*"

"To drill it into your head, Russell Cooper." She snapped out a dish towel and folded it in half. "'Ain't nothin' ain't gonna get you nowhere. 'Isn't anything' will."

I kept right on dusting.

She watched me a minute, then said, "What. You'd rather dust than improve your grammar?"

"I know how to speak proper, Mama. It just sounds off. Like it's somebody else talkin'." I wiped down the bookshelf and all the stupid baby pictures in between, and finally I grumbled, "There ain't no sense in dustin'. It all just comes right back again."

"Uh-huh," she said, folding a pair of my undershorts. "Same as laundry. But aren't you glad I don't make you run around in dirty undies?"

"Mama!"

She laughed, then said, "Go on. That's enough already. Go outside and be a boy."

I whooped and charged the door, then ran straight over to the Bankses'. Their car was in the drive, but not the truck. So I went right for the front door instead of knocking on Joey's window.

Joey's mama answered the door with a tired smile. "Why, hello, Rusty. Haven't seen you in two whole days. Where you been?"

"Been busy dustin'," I said, and tried to act cool. I'd been making myself scarce since we'd buried Smoky.

She laughed, and it made her eyes twinkle a little. "Dustin'? Boy, you can come visit here anytime if you give a hand in dustin'."

"Thanks, ma'am, but I'm tryin' to get *away* from all of that."

She opened the door wide and let me in. "I'll bet you are."

Rhonda saw me and cried, "Russy! Russy! Horsey! Horsey!" So I had to get down and play like a crazy wild mustang for a while before finding Joey in his room.

When I walked in, he flopped on his bed, looking guilty as sin. But then when he saw it was only me, he jumped right back up and told me to close the door.

I shut it tight and whispered, "Whatcha doin'?"

He stood on his bed with his ear to the wall. "They're up to something."

"Amanda Jane?"

He nodded. "And Jenna Mae."

I put my ear to the wall, too, but it seemed boring as fog to me. "They're just studyin', Joey."

"Shhh! I already missed part 'cause of all that racket you was makin' with Rhonda."

I listened some more, then sat down. "They're just studyin', Joey."

"Shoot," he said, and flopped on the bed. "They threw me out and blocked the door."

"And you think that's suspicious?"

"Don't be a smart-boy, Rusty."

"Well anyhow, I came over to see if you want to go down to the river."

"You kiddin'?" He jumped off the bed. "Let's go!"

The first thing we did was check out Smoky's grave. "Still packed in tight," Joey said.

"What were you expectin'?" I asked him.

He shrugged. "That maybe the Lost Ghost dug him up and had him for supper."

I wasn't going to let him get me spooked about the Lost Ghost. It's not like I actually *believed* those stories anyway. They were more for scaring little kids. So I said, "More'n likely he's floatin' around *with* the Lost Ghost, lookin' for mice."

Joey laughed. "You ain't scared 'cause it ain't dark yet. Just you wait."

We walked upstream, just talking stupid stuff. We skimmed rocks across the water and tossed frogs out for crappies. And it was fun. Fun just goofing around being boys.

And I did ask Joey about his dad and Smoky and if there was any news on that. All week at school he'd been nervous 'cause his dad suspected he'd had a hand in Smoky's disappearance, but now at the river he was joking around and acting like it was going to blow over.

The only one who knew for sure was me, and I wasn't gonna tattle.

Joey and me had a pact.

"Maybe you could get him another mouser. Make him forget about Smoky."

He hurled a rock across the river. "He can get his own dang mouser."

I shrugged. "Just a suggestion."

"He ain't even paid me for them squirrels yet. And you watch—I bet he don't. They were hoppin' with fleas once they cooled off, and now he's blamin' *me* 'cause there's fleas in the house. Stupid ol' Smoky had fleas galore, and since he ain't around for them to hop back on, they hop on Dad instead. But of course me and the squirrels get the blame."

"Did you bring the squirrels in the house?"

"No, stupid!"

"So they ain't your fleas . . . !"

"No kidding."

"Well that ain't fair!"

"Fair don't matter, Russ. When you gonna learn that?"

It wasn't long before I brought it up again. "Well if you get him a mouser, all the fleas'll hop on *him*, right?"

"Quit with that, Rusty-boy. I'm just glad I ain't slipped about Smoky. I can live with the fleas."

"What about the money he owes you?"

He shrugged. "I can live with that, too."

When we got up to the Lee Street Bridge, Joey pointed underneath and said, "That's where he lived."

"Who?"

"Jeremiah Vale—the Lost Ghost."

64   I scowled at him. "It ain't dark, Joey, and I ain't scared."

He looked at me all wide-eyed. "I ain't foolin' with you, Russ. I'm as serious as Smoky is dead. Jeremiah Vale lived right here. Folks say he was poorer'n pig tracks, and came to live down here after killin' his wife for food. And after he ate her all up, he turned to eatin' frogs and crappies . . . and little kids."

"Shut up, stupid."

"I swear to howdy it's true."

"Just quit with that, okay?"

He laughed. "Girls is so gullible with that."

"You brung *girls* down here?" Something about that seemed wrong. Like *that* was breaking a sacred pact.

"No!" He laughed again. "All's you gotta do is *tell* 'em about it and explain how you spent the night waitin' and watchin' for the Lost Ghost." His voice was all low and scary now, his eyes moving slow from side to side.

"Well have ya?"

"No! I don't believe in the Lost Ghost any more'n you! But if you tell the story all eerie-like, most girls get sucked in."

"You done that with girls at school?"

"Sure! And Amanda Jane, too."

"No! Amanda Jane? She don't *believe* you though, right?"

"She *says* she don't, but there's always an edge of fear in her eyes." He moved up the riverbank, laughing, "Oh, it's a joyful thing."

"To scare her?"

"Uh-huh. She's so uppity, y'know?"

"Uh-huh. Same as Jenna Mae."

We sat on the bank beside the bridge awhile, then just as we were fixin' to move on, the fattest, slimiest-looking frog you'd ever want to catch crept out of the water.

"Man, look at that!" Joey cried, running down to scoop him up.

But that frog took one look at Joey charging down the bank and *boiiiiing,* he jumped four feet up in the air. Maybe five!

"Dang!" Joey cried. "You see that?"

I laughed.

"Come help me, Russ!"

So we charged all up and down the bank, trying to nail that monster frog, and finally Joey dove for him and pinned him down with his chest.

"You didn't squish him, did you?" I asked, all out of breath.

"No! He's movin' good! I'll push up and you grab him, all right?"

"Me? I don't know . . . he's awful big."

"Don't be a wuss!"

"All right, all right!" I got down on my hands and knees while he pushed up, nice and slow. And the minute I could get my hands under, I grabbed that oversized polliwog around its big ol' belly and said, "Got him!"

"Man!" Joey said, getting up. "That thing's a tank! *Dang*, look at him!"

Its eyes were like little black marbles tucked inside rubbery green lids. It had bumps all over its back, and it felt cold and gooshy. "Here, Joey," I said. "You take him."

"Dang!" he said again, wrapping his hands around him. "Ain't *never* seen anything like him." Then all at once, something big and green and *squishy* came shooting out the frog's butt and ran down Joey's shirt.

The shock of it almost made Joey drop him, but he recovered in time. He laughed. "He's squishin' out green tomatoes!"

I laughed, too. "I think you scared the squishy green tomatoes *out* of him, Joey."

We admired the frog all around, and finally I asked, "So whatcha gonna do with him?"

"Keep him," he said.

"*Keep* him? How you gonna keep him?"

He gave me a loopy grin. "I'll figure something," he said, and headed up the riverbank.

8

TANK GOES TO SCHOOL

Joey decided he had the perfect place for Tank—Amanda Jane's underwear drawer.

I found out about it when I stopped by to pick him up for school the next morning. "You tryin' to get yourself *killed?*" I whispered when he told me.

He shrugged. "Dad ain't here. And Mama's already left with Rhonda. It's just me and Amanda Jane." He eyed me. "And, of course, you."

"I want no part in this, Joey."

"Don't be a wuss, Rusty. Look. I'll just say he got away. Whose fault is that?"

"Yours!"

"If you'd heard Amanda Jane last night, you'd be all for this."

"Why? What'd she say last night?"

"She was so snotty you wouldn't believe it. Even Dad had something to say about it."

"That bad?"

"Uh-huh." He grinned. "Dad thought Tank was pretty cool, by the way."

"He said so?"

"Uh-huh. Even Mama said I could keep him a couple days." He laughed. "And Rhonda wanted a froggie ride."

I laughed along with him, picturing Rhonda boinging around on Tank.

"But Amanda Jane? When I went down to her room to show her, she told me he was a slime-faced, turd-shaped pile of warts, and slammed the door on my foot." He stuck his toes in my face. "Hurt like hell."

"Ouch," I said, 'cause the second toe was scraped raw, and the nail was black and blue. "Looks like a crappie got it."

He took his foot back with a scowl. "Very funny, Rusty-boy."

"So when'd you put Tank in her dresser?"

"Five minutes ago. When she was in the john."

He dragged me into his room and put his ear to the wall. "What's she *doin'* in there?"

"Probably just messin' with makeup. That's what Sissy spends all morning doin'. That and fixin' her hair."

"How can you paint your face over three times and not change your underwear?" He plopped on the bed with a frown. "And I can't go to school without him."

"You're takin' Tank to *school?*"

"Not for pranks. Just to show off."

I started to tell him I thought that was a real bad idea, only first off, I knew he'd just call me a wuss again, and second off, right then the roof about shot off the house from Amanda Jane screaming, *"Eeeeeeeeeee! Aaaaahhhh!"*

"Ha-ha!" Joey cried, jumping up and down for joy. "Ha-ha!"

"Eeeeeeeeeeeeeek" came Amanda Jane's shriek through the wall. "Joey Banks, I hate you! I hate your guts, you hear me?"

Joey charged out of the room, crying, "You found him? Amanda Jane? Did you find Tank?"

I snuck along behind Joey and peeked into Amanda Jane's room. Tank was bouncing around all over the place. On the bed, off the bed. On the dresser, off the dresser. Joey was pouncing all around, trying to trap him.

"Where'd you find him?" he was saying. "I've been lookin' for him all mornin'!"

"You think I'm *stupid*? You think I don't know you planted that monster in my drawer? Wait 'til I tell Daddy! Wait 'til I—"

Tank jumped and landed on her head and stayed there, wrapping his squooshy green legs around her skull.

"Aaaaaaaaaaaaaaaaaaaaaaaaaaaagh!" she wailed, and when Tank shot off her he left squishy green poop running down the back of her hair.

She felt it there, and put her hand up to touch it. *"Aaaaaaaagh!* My hair's *ruined*." She ran into the bathroom but was back five seconds later. "If he pooped on my things . . ." She yanked open her top drawer. "There's green slime all *over* my things! It's . . . it's everywhere!"

"Hey, your hair and your things'll be fine," Joey told her. "Turds wash right out."

"I'm gonna get *warts* growin' on my head," she screamed. "I'm probably gonna get—" All of a sudden her eyes bugged out, then she whipped around and started digging through her underwear drawer. "I swear to God, Joey, if you took . . ." She slammed the drawer shut, then spun around and held a sharp breath. Her head started swayin' side to side. She looked deadly as a cornered snake. "Get out. Just get out!" she hissed. "And if I ever catch you in my room again, the rest of you will be wishin' it felt as good as your toe."

"Yes, ma'am," Joey said. He had Tank between his hands and was backing for the door. "Yes, *ma'am*. And I'll make sure Tank don't—"

She shoved him out and slammed the door. "I hate you, Joey Banks!"

Joey grinned a loopy grin. "Let's go, Rusty-boy."

Tank was too big for a pocket, that's for sure. So Joey gave him a quick soak in the sink, packed a bottle of water to use for keepin' him wet, then stuck him and a bunch of grass in a box. Then off we went. And true to his word, Joey didn't pull pranks at school. He just showed Tank off. And it was cool being with him, hearing him tell the tale of how we caught him.

The girls all *eeeew*ed and pinched up their noses, but the boys and teachers thought Tank was the coolest.

Every boy in school wanted to pick him up, only Joey told them all, "No chance! Besides, he'll squish poop all over you if you pick him up. Ask my sister. She got it all in her *hair* this morning."

"Eeeeeew!" squealed the girls.

"Cool!" laughed the boys.

Then Joey told the tale of Amanda Jane's underwear drawer and how Tank bounded clear to the ceiling escaping it. And as the day went by, the tale grew taller and taller, until all the kids were *begging* to see Tank jump.

So when school let out, Joey and me led the rest of the kids down to the field. Everyone circled around while Joey held Tank in the middle. "Step back," he called all around. "Farther! *Farther,* or he'll jump right over you!"

The circle widened, and finally Joey put Tank to the ground, still holding him around his belly. "Ready?" he called.

"Ready!" everyone called back.

"Are ya gonna touch him?" Joey hollered.

"No!" all the kids hollered back.

"Here goes!" He let loose and stepped back.

Nothing happened.

He took another step back.

Nothing happened.

"Go on, Tank!" he said.

Kids in the circle were starting to gripe.

"It ain't gonna jump."

"Look at it, just sittin' there!"

"What a dumb frog!"

Joey nudged him with his finger. "Go *on*, Tank, you're embarrassin' me."

Tank stayed put, blinkin' his eyes slow and careful, moving just his head from one side to the other.

"He's a brick, Joey!" a boy hollered from behind him.

"Yeah. A big green cow patty!"

"A wart wagon!"

Suddenly Tank shifted to the left and went *Boiiiiiing . . . Boiiiiiing . . . Boiiiiiiing!*

"Told you!" Joey cried, chasing after him. "Told you he was a big green kangaroo!"

The whole circle of heads followed after Tank, going up-down, up-down, up-down. *"Daaaaaang,"* the boys all cried. But Tank wasn't heading for boys.

He was heading straight for the only string of girls.

It was the strangest thing. It was like he aimed right for them. Like he knew they'd all squeal and let him through.

Which is exactly what they did.

"Close in," Joey cried. "Close in!"

About fifty boys pounced on Tank, and about forty-nine of them wound up with squishy green poop on them. But in the end, Joey got him back in the box and promised to bring him to school the next day, and we headed for home.

When we got to the corner of Pickett and Lee, I said,

"You know, Joey, you can't bring him back again. You gotta let him go."

"Why's that?"

"What's he eat?"

"Flies. Bugs. Nasty mosquitoes."

"You fed him any today?"

"Hmmm," he said. "Well, he's still poopin' good. Must mean he ain't totally depleted yet."

"Why don't we just put him back in the river? Catch him again some other day."

"Oh, like I'm ever gonna see this monster again once I let him go."

"Well, you can't keep him forever . . ."

"Well, I ain't done with him yet." He put the box down and took him out.

"What you doin' now?"

"I'm bettin' you."

"Bettin' me?" I asked him. "Betting me what?"

"That he can hop clean across Lee in one jump."

"What if a car comes by?"

"No cars is comin' by, Rusty-boy."

"They come by all the time."

"Well there ain't none coming by now. Besides, they gotta stop at the light."

"Not if it's green!"

"Don't be a wuss, Rusty. Are you in or not?"

"Not."

"Well, shoot. Just cross over and catch him then."

"No."

He gave me a disgusted look. "Fine. I'll do the whole dang thing myself."

But Tank wouldn't jump for Joey. He just sat there, blinking his big black eyes, moving his head slowly from side to side.

"He's thinkin', Joey. I swear, that frog's thinkin'."

"He's a bullfrog, Rusty. He don't think." He nudged him. "Any time, Tank. Do your thing."

Then a big blue pickup rumbled up Lee and came to a stop at the intersection. Joey grabbed Tank around his belly to hold him safe, but when the pickup pulled forward along Lee and was almost right in front of us, Tank twisted his head and bit Joey on the hand. And he bit him good, 'cause one minute Joey's got him around the belly, and the next he's wailing, "Owwww!" and letting go.

Then the most amazing thing happened. Tank jumped, *boiiiiiiing*, straight forward. And it looked like he was gonna splat right into the side of that truck, only he didn't collide with it. He landed smack-dab in the back of the bed, and stayed there, going along Lee, straight for the bridge.

"Wait! Come back!" Joey cried, running out into the street, flagging madly after the pickup. "You got my frog, mister! You got my frog!"

The pickup didn't even slow for him. It just rumbled along. And when it got to the Lee Street Bridge, Tank jumped again. I saw him, Joey saw him, but we ain't never told a soul about it 'cause folks all around would've called us nuts.

See, Tank jumped out of the pickup, clean over the guardrail, and I swear to howdy, we heard him land in the river.

That frog bummed himself a ride back home.

9

SISSY COOKS
HER OWN GOOSE

Amanda Jane and Sissy cornered us before we reached
Joey's house. They grabbed each of us by an ear and
dragged us along the blackberry thicket. "Owwww!" Joey
and I wailed. "Let go! Let *go*!"

"Hush up. Both of you just hush!" Amanda Jane hissed
and dragged us along even harder.

When they'd yanked us a good distance from the
road, they let go and stood over us with their arms
crossed tight. I figured we were in for it about Tank
messin' up Amanda Jane's drawer, but what Amanda
Jane said next confused me. Her eyes squinted down
to little slits, and she zeroed in on Joey. "In the first
place, I cannot believe you would snoop through my
things. I have *never* done that to you. In the *second*
place, if you breathe a word to Mama or Daddy, I'm
gonna tell them about you puttin' that slimy monster in
my drawer, about you swappin' out goldfish, and about
Smoky."

Joey's eyes shifted from side to side. "I ain't done
nothing with Smoky."

She snorted. "Oh, sure. Well I got a friend at school who owns a tracker."

"So?"

"So he says his dog can track down anything. 'Specially dead cats. All he needs is a whiff of Smoky and he'll find him. Dead or alive, six feet under, or washed up the river, he'll find him."

Joey laughed. "Tell him to come on, then. I ain't done nothing with Smoky."

Joey just stood there staring her down, and finally she looked away. So Sissy took up the fight. "Look. Amanda Jane ain't told on you about the goldfish, about the frog turds *or* Smoky. All we're askin' is for you to do the same. Fair's fair."

Joey speared me with his elbow before I could say something to give away that we had no *clue* what they were talking about. Then he said to his sister, "You ain't got nothin' on me. The goldfish is doin' just fine—"

"Thanks to *my* friend tellin' you how to fix things!"

"And Tank got loose, is all. Ain't my fault he found your drawer comfy."

"Liar! Liar-liar-liar!" Amanda Jane screamed at him. "You knew I wouldn't do nothin' about it! You knew—"

Sissy stopped her and pulled her aside. And while they had their heads together, whisperin' all frantic-like, I asked Joey, "You seen anything you weren't supposed to?"

"It was her *underwear* drawer, Rusty. I didn't exactly go snoopin'."

"There was somethin' in it. And she thinks you saw it."

"Some kind of female accessory?"

"Female accessory? What would that be?" I asked him.

"Who knows? Girls got all sorts of secret stuff, don't they?"

I thought about this, then said, "But why'd they be all bent outta shape about some female accessory?"

"Maybe our mamas don't know they're at that level of accessorizin'?"

I shook my head. "Ain't never heard of such a thing, Joey."

"Me neither."

"So it must be something else."

"Like . . . ?"

I shrugged. "Got me."

Amanda Jane and Sissy returned and sort of circled around, looking at us real suspicious-like. Finally Amanda Jane said, "We'll just call it even, okay? We won't tattle if you don't tattle."

I kept my mouth zipped while Joey looked from his sister to mine, cool as could be. Finally he said, "I ain't gonna tattle, Amanda Jane. Never planned to."

"Really?" she asked.

"Really," he said.

Everyone looked at me, so I just shrugged and said, "I

ain't gonna tattle," which was the truth—how could I tattle on something I didn't know?

"Well," Amanda Jane said, blinking away. "Then run along home!"

The minute we were alone, Joey said, "Shoot! I wish I'd dug through that drawer!"

"Me too."

"Shoot!"

Two days later I started figuring it out. Me and Dad were nosing through the refrigerator looking for something to eat, 'cause it was suppertime and we were both starved to death. Sissy and Mama hadn't even come *home* yet, and Dad was fluxing between his hunger and his worry. He hung on the refrigerator door, digging through leftovers, saying, "What do you suppose is keepin' them?" "Where do you suppose they are?" "Why do you suppose they haven't called?"

I wasn't worried. I was *hungry*. "What do you suppose we should *eat?*"

Then we heard them pull up the drive. Sissy came bounding out of the car carrying packages, Mama came bounding out of the car carrying supper.

"Who's in the mood for barbeque?" Mama cried as she sashayed through the door.

"Me!" I cried back, and tried to look in Sissy's packages. She snatched them back, so I asked her, "Whatcha got there?"

Mama beat her to the answer. "Two new outfits and a pair of shoes besides!"

Dad's eyebrows went up as he took the carryout from Mama. "Two new outfits?"

"It's all right, Jimmy, it's all right. Jenna Mae got an A on the Civil War exam!"

"She . . . did?" he asked, and his eyes bugged clean out. Sissy had never aced a test in her life.

"See, Jimmy? Jenna's *smart* when she puts her mind to it. She and Amanda Jane got the two highest scores in the whole entire school! Can you believe it?"

Sissy was back from dropping her packages in her room, so Dad said, "Well, congratulations, Jenna. I'm mighty proud of you."

"Thank you, Daddy." She helped Mama spread plates around, saying, "And believe me, it was hard! Like, when it'd give you a choice of years, it'd be 1861, 1862, 1863, or 1864. It was pickier than anything."

"Out of twenty-two pages—"

"Two hundred questions!" Sissy threw in.

"Jenna Mae only missed four," Mama said, beaming away.

"Only four?" Dad asked.

"Uh-huh," Sissy said as we all scooted up to the table. She served herself some pulled pork, then passed the carton to Dad, saying, "I'll bet *no* one got those four right."

Mama scooped out some butter beans and said, "See

what hard work and dedication will get you? Jenna Mae, I am just so proud!"

I looked at Sissy and could feel it in my bones—that girl had cheated.

After supper, I went over and looked in Joey's window. He was lying on his bed with his arms behind his head, staring at the ceiling. I gave our secret tap on his window, and he sprung out of bed and waved me around to the side door.

"I got it figured out, Joey," I told him when I was safe inside his room. "Amanda Jane and Jenna Mae cheated on that Civil War test."

"I was in here thinkin' the same thing. I just can't figure out how."

"Well, I can," I said, plopping on his bed.

"How?"

So I told him how Mama'd run off the tests upside down and backward, and had to rerun them.

"She took a copy home?"

"No! Mama'd never do that. Sissy and Jenna Mae *stole* one."

"How?"

"I'm guessin' they went back to the high school and dug one out of the trash."

"*Them* two? Dig through trash?"

"Better'n flunking, right? Which is what they woulda done if they'd taken it on their own."

"So all that studyin' they were doin' . . . ?"

"Was them lookin' up answers for a cheat sheet. Amanda Jane was most likely hiding the test in her underwear drawer."

"Daaaang," Joey said. "Beats the dirt out of anything I've ever done."

I shook my head. "We do somethin' and sweat it out for *days*. They do somethin' and get *rewarded*. Mama bought Sissy two new outfits, and a pair of shoes besides!"

"Yeah. And Amanda Jane gets a car."

"No!"

"I can't believe it either, but Dad said she deserved it, and Mama said it was about time anyhow. They already went through the ads and lined up a test-drive for tomorrow."

I felt like smacking the wall. "We gotta *do* something about it!"

He sighed. "I ain't riskin' Amanda Jane siccin' no tracker on Smoky."

"But it ain't fair!"

"Life ain't fair, Rusty-boy," he said, laying back on his bed with his arms behind his head. "Least that's what Dad always says."

The next morning, Sissy came out of her room in one of her new outfits. Mama told her she looked snappy. Dad said the same. I wanted to throw grape juice all over it.

Boy! Was I ticked off. And if it had been between just me and Sissy and my parents, I probably would have done something about it. But it wasn't just us. It was Joey, too. If I told on Sissy, she'd tell on Joey—which would turn out real painful at his end. So I just bit my lip and held my juice.

That afternoon, Sissy got a ride home in Amanda Jane's new car. "Dad took her out of school to buy it!" Joey whispered.

"It's kinda ugly," I whispered back. It was brown and big, with a bumper half off in back. "And why are they still sittin' in it?" They'd been parked out in front of the Bankses' since they got home, sorta bouncing around inside, giggling.

"'Cause she thinks it's the best thing ever. And shoot, you can see why. She got out of school to buy it!"

But when Mama got home that night, she wasn't bouncing around. Or giggling. Her lips were tight, and she barely said a word to anyone as she moved around the kitchen heating up leftover barbeque.

And when we were all sitting down for supper, she looked square at Sissy and said, "I had a very upsetting conversation with Mr. Hickle today."

"He's upsettin' *period*," Sissy said, heaping on beans.

"He accused me of providing you and Amanda Jane with a copy of the test."

Sissy's jaw dropped. "What on earth . . . ? That's the reward I get for studyin' so hard?"

Dad's face clouded over. "That takes a lot of nerve!"

"Amen to that," Mama said. "But he's aware that I'm

the one who ran off the test, and he's aware that prior to the test you were earning a D in the course." Sissy started to say something, but Mama put her hand up. "I told him I'd *warned* you—that I'd seen the test and knew it was tough—but that I would never, *ever*, do such a thing."

Dad was ready to thunder, but he held back. And Sissy's eyes were wide as saucers as she said, "He believed you, didn't he? I'll tell him myself tomorrow, if you want. I'll tell him how you said it was against your morals, and how you . . ."

From underneath the cushion on her chair, Mama pulled up a folded stack of papers. She said, "*However*, you did know I'd run the test off wrong. You did know there had to be bad copies in the school garbage. And"—she leveled a look at Sissy—"apparently you and Amanda Jane missed the same four questions."

Sissy just blinked at her.

"So I hope you don't mind putting my worries to rest by answering a few questions." Mama unfolded the papers and read, "What was the first state to secede from the Union? (a) Virginia, (b) Alabama, (c) Georgia, or (d) South Carolina."

"Mama, I cannot believe you're doin' this." Sissy turned to Dad. "Daddy? Do you find this as insultin' as I do? She don't trust me!"

Dad kept his eyes steady on Mama. "Just answer the question, Jenna Mae."

Sissy huffed and twitched and acted like she'd been

insulted clear to the moon, but didn't come up with an answer.

"Jenna Mae?" Mama asked her.

Sissy looked at her, then straight at me. And boy, if looks could kill, I'd be one dead doggie. I opened my eyes wide and moved my head a little side to side.

"Jenna!" Dad said. "Answer your mama."

For a second Sissy looked like a possum, lit up in the road. Then she blinked at Dad and snapped at Mama, "Well, repeat the question, then! You expect me to get it the very first time?"

So Mama did. "What was the first state to secede from the Union? (a) Virginia, (b) Alabama, (c) Georgia, or (d) South Carolina."

Wheels were spinnin' like mad inside Sissy's skull. "Virginia!" she said, all full of sass.

Mama looked at her and bit her lip.

Dad looked at Mama and said, "It's South Carolina, isn't it?"

Mama nodded at him.

"Well shoot!" Sissy said. "You got me all nervous, insultin' me like that. What do you expect?"

Mama went back to the paper. "Okay, well . . . What was Ulysses S. Grant doing when the war broke out? (a) Attending West Point, (b) Conferring with Abraham Lincoln, (c) Working in a leather shop, or (d) Vacationing in Maryland."

"Attendin' West Point!" Sissy shot out.

Dad shrugged.

I was clueless, too.

But Mama had the answers. "No, Jenna. He was working in a leather shop."

"So those must've been two of the ones I missed! Besides, you get your head chuck full of information for a particular *day*. When that day's over, you let it go. You expect me to go through my whole life with Civil War trivia stuck in my brain?"

Mama just ignored her and read from the paper. "In what state did the Battle of Fredericksburg take place? (a) Virginia, (b) Tennessee, (c) Mississippi, or (d) Pennsylvania."

"Which battle?"

"Fredericksburg."

"What states?"

"Virginia, Tennessee, Mississippi, or Pennsylvania."

Sissy straightened her posture. "Pennsylvania!"

Dad's eyebrow shot up. "Isn't it Virginia?"

Mama nodded.

"Everyone knows that . . . !" he said, looking disbelievingly at Sissy. "Even *I* know that."

"But, Daddy! I'm all panicked from the accusation! You can't expect me to *think* like this!"

Mama ran through about ten more questions.

Sissy got only one right.

"Enough," Dad finally said. "It's clear as day you cheated." His nose was flaring. His lips were tight. He hadn't touched his barbeque. "You are grounded, young lady."

"But, Daddy . . . !"

He stood halfway up and pointed a finger at her. "You're *grounded,* and . . . and I don't know what else. Your mama and I are going to have to discuss it."

Sissy started crying. "But, Daddy . . . it was an impossible test! Mr. Hickle's a war *nut.* Nobody could pass that thing!"

Mama folded up the test and let it drop to the floor beside her. "In addition to the disappointment and embarrassment, Jenna Mae, you might've cost me my job."

"Get those clothes your mama bought you and bring them here!" Dad hollered.

"But, Daddy!"

"Bring them here!"

Sissy got up, quivering. "But, Daddy, I wore an outfit to school today!"

Dad took a deep breath. "It'll be the last time you wear it, Jenna. And the rest is going back to the store."

"But—"

"*Get!*" Mama and Dad cried together.

Sissy brought the clothes out, then got sent back to her room without supper. Shortly after, Mama and Dad shoved back from the table and went to discuss things out on the porch.

Which left me and my growling stomach alone with a table full of scrumptious barbeque.

Some times life's more fair than others.

10

THE GHOST OF LOST RIVER

Mama was mortified, but she did not lose her job.

Sissy stayed grounded, couldn't ride to school or back with anybody but Mama, and had to take the Civil War test over again.

Amanda Jane must've done some fancy dancin' at home, though, 'cause she did *not* get grounded and got to *keep* her car. The only thing she couldn't seem to worm out of was retaking the test.

It wouldn't be the same test, either. Mr. Hickle was making up a brand-new one just for the two of them. "Bound to be twice as tough as the first one," Mama warned.

And that meant studying for real, but they weren't allowed to do *that* together, either. Oh, it would've been okay with Mrs. Banks, but Mama said no way.

Sissy did plenty of whining about it, saying how Mama and Dad were being overly hard on her, pointing out how Amanda Jane still had all her privileges, so why couldn't she?

Mama just counted to ten and said, "I can see the

lesson hasn't sunk in yet, Jenna Mae. When it does, we'll talk about privileges."

"But Amanda Jane's like my *sister*. You have no idea what this is doin' to me. She gets to go out and have fun, she gets to drive her very own car, she gets to—"

"Jenna Mae, go to your room!" Mama would shout, then mutter under her breath for half an hour.

The only time Amanda Jane and Sissy got to talk to each other was at noon-room duty. Aside from the humiliation of everyone finding out what they'd done, they were punished with trash duty for the final two weeks of school.

Needless to say, Sissy was in a permanent bad mood.

Now, Joey and me would've probably been in a permanent *good* mood if it wasn't for Amanda Jane's car. "It ain't fair!" Joey'd tell me when we'd see her zoomin' around. "So what if they can't return it. Least they ought to do is lock her out of it!"

Didn't stop *us* from having fun, though. We spent time hunting for Tank. Up the river, down the river. We probably covered ground a mile past the Lee Street Bridge. Maybe two. Distances are hard to tell when you're traveling along a riverbank. There's boulders and trees and other obstacles of nature slowing you down, warping yards into miles.

And every time we'd pass under the Lee Street Bridge, Joey'd try and scare me about the Lost Ghost, until finally I just told him, "Shut *up*, already. I ain't scared of no ghost."

He laughed and said, "I know you ain't, but lots of folks *is*, and I aim to keep that goin'."

"Why?" I asked him. "For when you bring *girls* down here?"

"No, Rusty-boy!" But then he snapped his fingers, loud as anything.

"What?"

"I got an idea!"

"What? What idea?"

He ran back out from underneath the bridge and looked up and all around.

"What, Joey? Whatcha thinkin'?"

"Follow me!" he cried, and tore off under the bridge.

When we came out the other side, he looked all around. He ran up the bank to the road, tested a tree branch that was hanging overhead, looked up and down Lee Street, then tore back down to the river, looking up, looking over . . . looking *everywhere*. Finally he planted himself right in front of me and gave me his loopy grin. "Rusty-boy, *we're* gonna be the Lost Ghost."

"Huh? How do you mean?"

"Come on!" he said, charging up to the street. "I'll tell you on the way home!"

That night we met up again outside Joey's back door. He had a sack of supplies and was already waiting when I arrived. "They know you're out?" he whispered.

I shook my head. "I snuck out my window, just like you said."

"Stuffed your bed?"

"Uh-huh."

"Good. Let's go!"

We tore down to the river and over to the bridge. It was black as pitch out, too. No moon, no stars. Just thick river air and darkness.

Lee Street was deserted. We could see the stoplight where Tank had bummed a ride home, but up Lee the other way was like a tunnel of blackness.

"We ain't gonna spook no one if the road's deserted," I told Joey.

"We *want* it to be deserted while we're settin' up, Rusty-boy. Come on! Let's get the rope up."

It wasn't exactly rope. It was more heavy string. And it took a lot of hurlin' to get it over the branch right. There we were, in the middle of the road, tossing a ball of string back and forth like it was opening day, Joey talking the whole time. "Higher, Rusty!" "Shoot! It's too far over." "Pull it down!" "Okay, now catch!" "Shoot!"

It took us forever to get it just where Joey wanted, and when he finally said, "That's *perfect*," headlights came over the rise and out of the tunnel of darkness.

We dove under the bridge, but in doin' so we pulled the string clean out of the branch. "Shoot!" Joey said when the car passed and we saw the string laying on the street like a giant noodle. "We got to start all over again!"

This time we got it looped over the branch quicker,

though, 'cause Joey decided not to be so picky. Then we ducked under the bridge and started fixing up the ghost.

Now, Joey hadn't exactly told me *how* we were gonna make the ghost. He just told me to meet him. So when I saw him blowing up a balloon I said, "Joey! Nobody's gonna fall for that!"

"Just hold on, all right, smart-boy?" He pinched off the air. "You'll see."

He stuck the balloon inside a black pillowcase, and I couldn't help asking, "Black? Ain't ghosts supposed to be white? And where'd you get a black pillowcase, anyhow?"

He rolled his eyes. "I tried white in my room. It looked fake. Black's *way* better. And don't ask me—it was in the closet."

Next he put his flashlight inside the pillowcase, turned it on, and pinched the case around the base of the light end. "See?" he whispered, holding it up.

"Hey . . . that's good," I said.

"Told ya."

We tied a piece of string around the Lost Ghost's neck so the balloon and the top of the flashlight were both stuck inside the head. Then Joey stapled on some tattered jeans so they hung down from inside the pillowcase.

"Jeans, Joey? You think the Lost Ghost wears jeans?"

"He does now, Rusty." He tied one end of the tree rope through the neck rope and said, "He's gotta be big enough to notice, don't he?"

Joey switched on the light and hoisted him up the tree

branch, and I had to admit—he was one fine-looking ghost. "Say," I whispered. "That's scary!"

"Told ya!"

About three cars had gone whizzing by while we were fixing up the Lost Ghost. They hadn't seen us 'cause we were doing everything down the hill. But now we were ready, crouched low beside the bridge, Joey holding tight to the string. "Whatcha fixin' to do?" I asked him.

"I'm gonna do like this," he said, letting out the string. The Lost Ghost came down from the tree, slow and scary.

"Cool!" I whispered.

He gave me a loopy grin and hoisted it back up. "Told ya!"

About two minutes later, a car came up Lee from the stoplight. And as it zoomed up the hill toward the bridge, Joey whispered, "We're gonna scare the bazooka out of him! We're gonna make him run home to mama! We're gonna . . ."

"Hush up, Joey! Here he comes!"

Joey let the Lost Ghost down real slow and scary-like. But the car just barreled by without slowing.

"Dadgumit!" Joey said, hoisting the ghost back up. "I don't think he even saw it!"

"Maybe you gotta let it down quicker?"

"Yeah. Quicker and lower." He pointed to headlights coming out of the darkness. "Get ready!"

"Maybe it's the same guy. Maybe he flipped a U-ie. Maybe he's gonna—"

"Hush up yourself, Rusty!"

He dropped the ghost quicker and lower, and it *wasn't* the same car, but it did the same thing—just kept on driving.

"Maybe I gotta drop it and yank it back up as they go by."

We waited probably five minutes, but it felt like an hour. And when we spotted headlights coming out of the darkness down Lee, Joey cried, "Here's one now! Come on, car, I'll show ya . . . the Lost Ghost lives!"

The minute the car hit the bridge, Joey let out his bundle of slack. The Lost Ghost fluttered down fast, then Joey yanked it up and away.

"You practically hit the windshield, Joey!"

Before the words were even out of my mouth, the car swerved and started fishtailing all over the place. It spun out of control toward the stoplight, smoke coming from the brakes, sparks coming from who knows where. And as I saw it heading straight for a phone pole, my heart froze in my chest.

"Uh-oh," Joey whispered as it crashed into the pole. "Uh-*oh*."

Then headlights from a car coming up the hill lit up the crashed car, and that's when Joey said what I was seeing but not believing. "That's Amanda Jane's car . . . !"

"Can't be," I whispered.

"It *is*. Oh maaaaaan! She's gonna tattle! And you watch—I'm gonna pay for that old clunker with my hide." He shook his head. "Boy, that Amanda Jane's an awful driver!"

The other car had stopped to help, and almost right away after, there was a third car pulling up to the crash.

I wanted to run down to help, too, but Joey grabbed my shirt and dragged me back. "There's plenty of folks there already. What we gotta do is get the ghost down. Get it down quick."

There were folks all over Amanda Jane's car, and it didn't seem that us joining them would do any good. So I helped Joey cut the ghost down and pull everything under the bridge.

Joey popped the balloon and shoved all the stuff back in the pillowcase, saying, "Dad can*not* find out about this, Rusty. If he does, he's gonna kill me. He's gonna beat me to a inch of my life, then beat me some more."

I chased after him under the bridge and along the river, saying, "Maybe Amanda Jane'll think it *was* the Lost Ghost. Your parents don't know you snuck out, right?"

"If they do, I'm doomed. I'm dead. It'll all be over but the cryin' . . ."

Then we heard sirens in the distance, and Joey said, "The cops are comin' already!"

He stumbled down to the river and started to fling the pillowcase in, but I grabbed it in time. "No, Joey! It'll just float up to shore. You gotta take it and put it all back where you found it." The sirens were getting louder. "Just get yourself back in bed before they notice you're gone!"

But before we split up to go our own ways, Joey stopped me and said, "I swear to howdy, if you tell a soul . . ."

"I *won't*, Joey! Don't you know that by now?"

He opened his knife, skipped the fists, and went straight for blood. And when we'd rubbed our fingers together good, he whispered, "You're my friend, Rusty. My true friend."

"You're mine, too," I told him.

Then we hurried home to creep through our windows and shake in our sheets.

11

BLACKBERRY MUD

When they told me Amanda Jane was dead, I went into cold, hard shock. I didn't believe it. I *wouldn't* believe it. My family just shivered on the street in our pj's along with the rest of the block, listenin' to folks say how horrible it was.

Joey's mama had been the alarm that had woken up the neighborhood—screamin' and wailin' and runnin' in circles, cryin', "Not my baby! Not my baby!"

But it was true. And while Joey's mama and dad followed the ambulance into town, Joey and Rhonda stayed with us, Joey and me shiverin' the night away on the floor of my room.

At four in the morning I saw his eyes wide open, staring out the window. "What are we gonna do?" I whispered.

He just shook his head.

Mama made sticky buns for breakfast, but it was hopeless. No one ate. Sissy's eyes were puffed nearly closed, and she wound up going back to her room to cry 'em out some more.

Mrs. Banks came and fetched Rhonda and Joey in the morning, and tried to fight back the tears as she told us how a mechanic had checked the car over and found the brakes to be faulty. "If only we'd bought her a better car," she said as she broke down in Mama's arms. "If only she'd been wearing her seat belt!"

Dad was real solemn. And I know he and Mama were both thinking about what it would be like to lose your girl like that. And that, if not for the grounding, Sissy might've been in that car, too.

A short while later, Joey was back, knocking on the door. Said he couldn't take being in his own house. Mama tried to say soothing things to him. "She's in heaven now," she told him. "It'll be some time, but you'll see her again." She patted his hand. "Then you can take up fightin' with her from where you left off."

Normally that would've made Joey laugh—which was what Mama was tryin' to get him to do—but now he just looked down and shook his head.

It was the slowest day in existence. Sissy cried. Joey and me sat and shivered in my room. None of us went to school. Mama cooked a casserole to take to the Bankses. Dad went to work, but didn't stay long. He came home and offered to take us out. "Anywhere," he said. "Anywhere you want to go."

Sissy kept on cryin'. Joey and me shook our heads, and

we went back to my room, where Joey finally said the words. "I killed my own sister," he whispered. "I killed Amanda Jane."

"You did not," I whispered back. "It was an accident, is all. You heard your mama saying how the brakes on that car were no good, and that Amanda Jane should've been wearin' her safety belt. It was an accident, Joey. An accident."

He just shook his head.

I was trying to make him feel better, but my stomach wasn't buyin' it, either. If there'd been any food in it at all, it would've come up right then and there.

Every time there was a knock on the door, we'd scramble to the window, sure the police were on to what we'd done. But the police didn't come. Not that day, or the next. Or the day kids from the high school brought a truckload of plastic flowers to the crash site and nailed a white cross to the phone pole. The cross had AMANDA painted in pink down the length and JANE painted across.

No police showed up at the funeral either. Or later at the graveyard, where we watched her coffin get lowered into the ground.

It was my first funeral, and I'm hoping it'll be my last. Folks cryin' all over. Everyone in black. The minister dronin' on about a lovely flower being plucked from the earth, joinin' the everlastin' bouquet at the good Lord's side.

But what really got me was Joey's dad. He bawled his

eyes out. Worse even than Joey's mama, who was trying to be strong for Joey and Rhonda.

Summer came and sweltered on. Mama got Sissy counseling 'cause she hadn't stopped crying. Joey and me were still walking around like zombies. We tried going down to the swimming hole. Tried looking for Tank. But everything reminded us. The bridge. Smoky's grave. Everything.

Dad tried to get me to talk about things, but I wouldn't. I *couldn't*. I had a pact with Joey. And besides, who wants to tell their dad they're an accomplice to murder?

Every time I passed by the phone pole cross, I felt like puking. Every time I saw Joey's mama, I felt like crying. Every time I heard Sissy bawling in her pillow, I wanted to beat myself silly for not thinking things through.

How come we never thought someone might get hurt?

When school finally started up again, I was hoping things would change, but they didn't. Joey and me just sat. Not listening. Not talking. Not caring.

Three weeks into the school year, Mama showed up in the middle of the day and pulled me from class. She stuck me in the car and started driving.

"Where we goin', Mama?"

She kept her eyes fixed on the road. "Your daddy and I have been so concerned about Jenna Mae for all her cryin' that we didn't realize how deeply Amanda Jane's death was affecting you."

"I'm okay, Mama."

101

"No, you're not. According to the school, you're seriously not."

"But, Mama . . ."

Her eyes were brimming with tears now, and she gripped the wheel tighter. "Honey, you don't eat, you don't sleep, you don't cry, you don't talk . . ." She glanced my way. "Look at those bags under your eyes. Look at you sitting there shivering!"

"But, Mama . . ."

"Just give her a chance."

"Who?"

"The counselor."

"Sissy's counselor?"

She nodded. "She knows a lot about what's going on already."

"But—"

"Honey, sometimes it helps to talk to someone you don't know."

Dr. Louise was nice enough, but I didn't talk to her, either. Not that day, or the next, or the one after that. She tried to get me to play with little figures, tried to get me to move little magnet people around a board, tried to get me to talk about my feelings. But I just sat there, staring at my feet.

Joey and me had a pact.

Sealed for life.

Finally she said, "Russell? If you keep it buried, it's going to rot."

I thought about Amanda Jane, restin' six feet under. "Fine choice of words, ma'am."

She caught my meaning and hurried to say, "What I'm trying to tell you, Russell, is if you keep it bottled up too long, you'll destroy yourself from the inside. You've got to let it *out*."

"Yes, ma'am."

She sat there, blinking at me for an eternity. "Well?"

"Well what, ma'am?"

"Aren't you going to try and let it out?"

I just shrugged and looked down.

Joey wasn't getting over it, either. He took to cutting school. He'd come one day, then be gone for three. He didn't want to walk around, didn't want to talk. He just wanted to be left alone.

Which I understood. Seeing him reminded me, too.

I thought back on my first year with Joey Banks. And I wished with all my might that things could be that way again. But the scary part was, things weren't returning to the way they'd been.

They seemed to be getting worse.

Then one night there was a tap on my window. The secret tap. And when I pulled back the curtain, there was Joey, giving me a loopy grin from right outside.

I pulled on my jeans and climbed out, whispering, "What you got there?" 'cause he had a clear plastic sack with something dark and sloshy-looking inside.

"Come with me," he said, still grinning.

So I followed him down to the river, wondering what in the world he was up to, and why he was walking so funny, kinda staggering around. "What is it, Joey? Where we goin'?"

"You gotta try this," he said, raising the plastic bag a little. "It makes ya feel a *whole* lot better."

"What *is* it, Joey?"

He tossed me a loopy grin over his shoulder. "Blackberries."

"Blackberries?"

"Uh-huh."

We got down to the swimming hole, and I followed Joey up to our favorite rock. The moon was shining overhead, and the water looked sparkly. Cool and clear and pure. It had been ages since we'd been there together, and I stared into the water for a full minute, feeling like there was a noose strangling my heart.

Finally, I shook it off and sat beside Joey, saying, "Whadda ya mean, blackberries? Looks like mush to me."

He took two paper cups out of his pocket and handed them over. One was already stained purple. "Here, hold these. I'll fill 'em."

"I ain't sure I want to eat blackberry mush."

"We ain't eatin', Rusty-boy," he said as he untied the bag. "We's *drinkin'*."

It was so nice to hear him call me Rusty-boy again that it didn't occur to me right off what he was saying. I just held a cup out and let him pour. "Blackberry juice?" I asked him. "From your thicket?"

"Uh-huh." He filled up the other cup. "But it ain't exactly *juice*, either."

I sloshed it around in my cup. "Looks like *mud*, if you ask me."

He threw back his head and laughed. "Only mud around here's in your head." He took a big gulp, and smiled at me. "Go on, drink!"

So I did. And the minute it hit my lips, I spit it out. "Awwww! That's *awful*."

"But it sure makes you feel good." He gulped back some more. "And ya quit tastin' it after a while."

His teeth were glowing purple in the moonlight, and all of a sudden he looked kinda wild to me.

Kinda crazy.

"Try it again, Rusty-boy. You'll see."

I sniffed the cup. "It's . . . wine?"

"Uh-huh." He poured himself a refill.

I just held on to my cup and watched him down some more. "I'm not sure this is such a hot idea, Joey."

"Nothin' we do's a hot idea. Ever notice that? Everything we touch dies. Crappies, goldfish, ground squirrels, cats, *sisters*. . . ." He took another gulp. "We's killin' machines, Rusty-boy!"

"That ain't true," I said quietly. "How about Tank? He's out there gettin' fatter'n a hog, squishin' green tomatoes all over the place!"

He snickered. "Yeah. We's dumber'n frogs. Can you believe that? If we'd've been *smarter'n* frogs, he'd be dead, too. Guaranteed."

We sat there quiet for the longest time. Him gulping down mud, me looking into the water. Finally I asked, "Your mama makin' you see a counselor?"

He snorted. "Na."

"Mine is."

He looked at me, and suddenly there was worry in his eyes.

"No, Joey, I ain't told, and I ain't *gonna* tell."

He went back to drinkin' fermented mud. The bag was nearly empty.

"The counselor says if I don't talk about things it'll rot me from the inside out."

He didn't say a word. Didn't look at me. Just threw back some more mud.

"I think that might be what's happenin' to us, Joey," I told him, barely above a whisper.

He slammed down his cup. "Well, what else we suppose' to do? Dad would murder us! You should hear him sobbin' at night. Mama, too! She looks horrible and forgets where she is half the time! And if Dad *don't* kill us, the cops'll throw us in jail, and someone in jail'll do us in. Jails is horrible places, Rusty. I've heard all about 'em and I ain't goin' to no *jail*." His words were fallin' all over each other, getting tangled and tripped up. Then, all of a sudden, Joey started crying.

"Hey," I said, 'cause I didn't know what else to say. "Hey, hey."

But he kept on crying and finally said, "She used to do horsey for me! Jus' like you do with Rhonda? When we was little she used to do horsey."

"Amanda Jane did?" I just couldn't picture it.

"Uh-huh. An' she used to tell me stories in bed about Bunny Boy."

"Bunny Boy?"

"Uh-huh. He was this little rabbit that was friends with all the forest animals and had a magic box."

"What sort of magic box?"

"Bunny Boy would put in snakes and turn 'em into butterflies. He'd put in fish and they'd come out with wings. Flyin' fish, all over the forest!" He was sobbing now. Hiccuping and sputtering so that I could barely understand him when he said, "I loved Bunny Boy!"

I started crying, too, 'cause I knew what he was really saying was that he loved Amanda Jane.

Then suddenly Joey quit sobbing, and his eyes got all big as he teetered back and forth, back and forth.

Then he got up on his knees, leaned over the rock, and puked his purple guts out.

12

BREAKING POINT

When I snuck back through my window, I had a big surprise waiting.

My dad.

About gave me a heart attack when I saw him sitting on my bed, arms crossed, face scrunched together like an angry cloud. And I thought for sure heated words were gonna rain all over me, but all he did was sit there watching me fumble around.

"I . . . I'm sorry, Dad," I said.

His mouth twitched. His foot twitched. His angry-cloud face looked likely to roll with thunder. But all he said was, "For . . . ?"

"For sneaking out. Sir."

He nodded, still twitchin' and rollin' inside with thunder. "And . . . ?"

"And . . . and being deceptive. Sir!"

Mama walked in, wrapped tight in her robe. Dad shooed her out without a word. I just stood at attention, shaking in my shoes.

"Explain yourself, Russell Cooper. And it better be good."

"Yes, sir. Yes, sir!" I said. "Joey and me was down at the river—"

"You plan this out?"

"No! No, sir! He tapped on my window and—"

"You ever snuck out like this before?"

I looked down, remembering the night of the Lost Ghost. The night Amanda Jane died. "Yes, sir." Then I added, "But mostly he taps when he wants *in*. You know—when it's too late to knock on the door 'cause it'll wake everyone up."

More thunder was gathering, I could see it. But he drew in a deep breath and said, "What did the two of you do tonight? Down at the river."

"We talked, mostly. Joey's all messed up over Amanda Jane. He ain't been talkin' to me at *all*. So tonight when he tapped, I went with him." I shrugged. "He's my friend, y'know?"

"Friends can sometimes lead friends down the wrong path, son."

My knees were locked tight, keeping me up, but the minute he said "son," they started wobbling. Just shaking away like crazy. His voice was softer, and the angry cloud was dissipatin'. Not gone entirely, but moving slowly across the horizon. And at that instant I about broke down and told him everything. Everything about Amanda Jane.

Only I thought of Joey and the pact we'd made and how it wouldn't do a lick of good to tell Dad about it.

It would only make things worse.

So instead, I nodded and looked down.

"You two been smokin'?"

"No, sir!"

"Drinkin'?"

"No, sir!" Then I added, "At least not me, sir." And I didn't feel bad about saying it. Joey and me hadn't made a pact about that one.

Dad's eyebrows shot up. "Joey was?"

"Yes, sir. And I did try a little, but I spit it right out. Tasted terrible."

"What was he drinking?"

"Blackberry mud, if you ask me."

"What's that?"

"Fermented blackberries, sir."

"Blackberries from his thicket?"

"Yes, sir."

He frowned, but it wasn't a terrifying one. "He's got a never-endin' supply of those back there, don't he?"

"Yes, sir."

He sat there, checking me over, twitching at the face. "Walk, Russell. From there, to over there," he said, pointing across the room.

My knees were weak and wobbly, but they got me across okay.

"Close your eyes and do like this," he said, bringing his first fingers together.

So I did, only my fingers missed each other completely.

"Try it again," he said.

This time they touched.

"Spin in a circle three times."

"I only had a sip!"

"Spin!"

I spun, boy. Like a top.

"Let me smell your breath."

I huffed in his face. Then I backed up and said, "Dad, I swear, I had a teaspoon and spit it out."

He nodded, but was still not happy. He said, "But if it had tasted *fine*, you'd've drunk it up, am I right?"

I shrugged and looked down. "I told him I didn't think it was a hot idea . . ."

"But you went along with it anyway."

"He was *talkin'*, Dad. For the first time in ages, Joey was talkin'."

His cheeks puffed up like one of those pictures you see of the North Wind, blowin' clouds across the sky. Then he let his breath out, long and steady, and said, "Your mama and I have tried everything in this world to get *you* to talk, son. And you may as well know that we're mighty frustrated, throwing away money on a counselor that can't get more'n a peep out of you. Your mama's convinced you need to talk, your counselor says you're keeping something dark inside, and I don't know what to do about any of this. Part of me thinks you deserve a good whuppin' for what you did tonight, but part of me's relieved that you had the sense not to come home staggering drunk." He eyed me. "Is that the state Joey's in?"

I nodded. "Yes, sir. He's sicker'n a dog."

Dad shook his head and muttered, "Wonder what his daddy'll do when he finds out."

I shuddered, and all of a sudden my knees felt like jelly again. "Dad?"

"Yes, son."

"Thanks for not whuppin' me."

He nodded.

"I promise I won't sneak out no more."

He nodded again, then let loose a heavy sigh. "That's what I want to hear, son." He gave me half a smile. "And I've never known you to break a promise."

I looked at him, then looked down. "Yes, sir."

He got up and put his hand on my shoulder and said, "I know this business with Amanda Jane has been tough on you. It's been tough on all of us." He looked at me. "Is the counselor helping *any*?"

I shrugged. "Maybe. But probably not. Didn't know you were *payin'* her, Dad."

He snorted. "Same as any other doctor."

"Well." I shrugged again. "I wouldn't pay her no more if I was you."

He sighed and said, "I want you to know that your mama and I are here. No matter when, no matter what. If you want to talk, we'll do our best to listen."

My chin quivered. "Yes, sir."

He started for the door, but turned and said, "You got something you want to say to me now?"

My chin was still quiverin', and it felt like a giant lump of grits was stuck in my throat. I shook my head. "No, sir."

I couldn't stop thinking about Joey. About how he'd nearly puked his guts into the river, emptyin' out the blackberry wine. About how he'd sat on the rock and bawled like a little baby, rocking back and forth, back and forth. About how I'd had to practically pour him through his window to get him back into the house, and how he'd just curled up in a ball on the floor starin' off into nowhere while I eased the window closed behind him.

And after staring at my own ceiling for nearly an hour, I still couldn't shake the picture of him, so miserable and pained by what had happened.

I thought about sneaking out the window. All I wanted was to check on him quick, then get back to bed. But I'd made a promise, so I went and woke Dad up instead.

"Huh?" he asked, lookin' up all groggy. "Russell, what is it?"

"Just wanted to let you know I'm goin' over to check on Joey," I whispered, quiet as I could.

"Check on Joey?" Mama sat up straight as a church pew. "Now?"

"Sorry, Mama. Didn't mean to wake you."

"Why you checkin' on Joey now?" Dad asked, looking at the clock. "He's gotta be out cold."

"I can't shake the picture of him cryin' on his floor. I just want to go peek in his window."

They gave each other a shrug, then Dad said, "Go on, then. But hurry right home."

I nodded. "I'll be right back."

The moon was like a powerful flashlight, lighting the path from our house to Joey's. I raced over quick as a rabbit, and was expecting to just peek in and dash home, only when I looked in Joey's window, my heart froze cold.

Joey was sitting up in bed, cross-legged, with the muzzle of his .22 stuck straight in his mouth.

I almost pounded on the window, but I was scared the noise would make him set off the gun. His thumb was stuck through the lever, smack-dab against the trigger. "Joey!" I called through the glass. "Joey, no!"

His eyes roamed over to the window.

"Joey, don't!" I said, shaking my head like crazy.

I know he saw me, but his eyes drifted away, then stared straight ahead.

So I lifted the window and pulled myself inside, saying, "Don't do it! *Don't!*"

He took his mouth off the muzzle long enough to say, "Don't be a wuss, Russ. There ain't no other way out."

"I *ain't* a wuss, Joey," I cried, diving for the gun. "I'm your friend!"

The instant I landed, the gun went off, blasting a hole right through the wall. And before we could finish shouting at each other, Joey's dad came crashing through the door like a wild bear. "What the *hell*'s goin' on in here?" he roared.

"Nothin'!" Joey cried.

"He was tryin' to *kill* himself is what's goin' on!" I yelled. Then I snatched up the gun and hurled it out the window.

Joey's mama was in the room now, too. "What?" she cried. "What did you say?"

"Outta here, woman!" Joey's dad hollered at her, then came at us, muttering, "Looks like we got a coward for a son."

His head was lollin' a bit, and his steps were staggerin'. Like his body was trying to sleep while the rest of him was hungry for blood.

Before he could lay a hand on either of us, I grabbed Joey by the wrist and yanked him with me over the bed, out the door, down the hall, and out of the house. And I kept on yankin' him, across his yard, then mine, as I hollered at the top of my lungs, "Daaaad! Dad, come quick! Daaaaad!"

Joey's dad was behind us, shouting, "Get back here, boy! Get back here now!"

Mama and Dad were already on the porch, looking paler than the Lost Ghost. "What's going on? Russell, what happened?"

Sissy was out on the porch now, too, wrapped in her robe, and Joey's mama was racing our way, crying, "Bobby! Bobby, stop!"

"Get home, woman!" he hollered back at her. "Get!"

My heart was thumpin' like a trapped rabbit's. My knees were wobbly as noodles. But I held on to Joey tight and called off the porch, "You ain't touchin' him, mister! You ain't layin' a hand on my friend!"

Mama whispered, "Russell, what is going *on?*"

"Joey was about to shoot himself with his twenty-two."

"On *purpose?*" Mama asked.

"Shut up!" Joey hissed. "If you're my friend, you'll shut up right here and now."

"I *am* your friend, and I *ain't* shuttin' up." I looked at the faces all around us. Then I looked at Joey and knew we couldn't go on the way we'd been going on. So I took a deep breath and said, "Yes, on purpose."

"Why?" Joey's mama asked through her tears.

"Don't!" Joey cried, trying to break free.

But I shoved him in a porch chair and held him down with all my might. "'Cause Joey and me's responsible for Amanda Jane's crash, that's why!"

Air sucked into mouths all around. There was a horrible moment of complete silence, then Sissy cried, "You?" and Mama gasped, "How?" and Joey's mama wailed, "What?" while my dad and Joey's dad took steps toward each other.

"Tell us what happened," Dad said as soon as he was sure Joey's dad wasn't gonna storm the porch. "What did the two of you do?"

So I let it all out about the Lost Ghost and the prank

we'd pulled and how we didn't mean to hurt no one—how we were just out to have a little fun. Then I said, "Only things took a horrible turn and now Amanda Jane's dead and Joey and me's tortured over what we done, to the point where Joey's gonna do himself in 'cause he don't see no other way out."

"Oh, Joey!" Mrs. Banks cried, running up the porch to hold him. "Oh, my Joey!"

Joey started to break down, but then his dad came stomping up the steps. "This boy killed our girl and you're gonna give him *sympathy?*" He pushed past Dad, but I stepped right in his way and hollered, "Don't you touch him! It ain't right the way you—"

He pushed me aside like a branch in his way, but Dad wedged between them and puffed himself up. "Bobby, you'd best take a deep breath and a step back from this."

"Don't you tell me how to treat my kid, Cooper. He's *my* kid."

"And this here's my porch, and there's not gonna be any fightin' on it, you got that?" Dad was looking steelier than I'd ever seen, holding his ground against one bear of a man.

Joey's dad stared my dad down for a whole minute before turning to Joey's mama and sayin', "Get him home, woman."

"No!" she said, flinging tears aside. "Not until you calm yourself and swear to me you won't touch him."

"He killed our little girl, you got that? You expect him to go unpunished?"

She stood up and screeched, "Don't you see? We almost lost *him* tonight, too! You never *listen*, Bobby! You just storm off or hit! We can't go on like this, you hear me? Things have gotta change!"

Mama reached out and gave her back a calming rub. Joey's eyes were big as flapjacks. Sissy was blinkin' like mad, and Dad was still holding his ground between Joey and his dad.

Finally Joey's dad said, real quiet-like, "Get back to Rhonda."

"No! Rhonda is fine."

"I said get!"

"And I said no!" She turned to Mama, and they had some silent magical female conversation, which resulted in her looking back at her husband and saying, "I'm staying here. All of us are stayin' here 'til you cool off."

Joey's dad stood there another minute or so, then turned around and stormed back to the house.

I started worrying about him returning with a gun, and Dad was thinking the same, 'cause he got his ready and carried it with him from room to room as we set things up for the night. I think Dad would've called the police, only Mama and Joey's mama were having trouble deciding what to do about everything. If the police found out what we'd done, would they file charges? Would we get sent to juvenile hall? Would we have records? What were they gonna do about what we'd done?

So our mamas sat up talking, Dad sat by the door with the gun across his lap, and Sissy spent half her time crying and the other half shouting nasty things at us. And somewhere in the middle of all that, Joey fell asleep on his mama's lap, and I fell asleep on the floor.

And for the first time since Amanda Jane died, I slept clear through to morning.

13

SENTENCED

Living next door to the Bankses was tough after that. Awkward. And I wound up playing that night back in my head, over and over and over. Maybe I should've done things different. Maybe Joey really *wasn't* gonna pull the trigger after all. Or maybe he *did* really believe he'd have been better off dead. He said both things inside an hour, so it's hard to know.

Either way, he told me, I'd broken a sacred pact, and we were through.

For a while, our parents had the same problem Joey and me had. Should they tell the police? Or should they keep it within our families. "After all," Joey's mama said, "everyone whose business it is already knows."

But after a couple of days it became real clear that it wouldn't stay a secret for long. Sissy was madder'n a wet hen. At me, at Joey, at Mama and Dad for *not* bein' mad at me . . . There was no way that girl was gonna keep her mouth shut about what we'd done.

"Besides," Mama said when she and Dad told me they and Joey's mama had decided to tell the police. "There's nothing they can do to you that's worse than the sentence you've already got."

Amen to that. Part of me *wanted* them to toss us in the slammer and throw away the key. Would beat feelin' the way I'd been feelin', that's for sure.

But after they heard the whole story, the police just let us go. Nobody was pressing charges, they said. Nobody outside our families had been hurt. They wound up shutting the case a lot quicker than we'd opened it.

At least *legally* that's what happened. School was a different story. Word got out, all right, and kids took to treating us like we were diseased. They didn't know what to say, so they avoided us altogether, which was harder to take than if they'd said mean things to us.

So instead of going to jail, Joey and me had the back-to-back tortures of staying in school and living right next door to each other.

School I could have handled if I'd had Joey at my side. But he'd have nothing to do with me, so I spent my days alone, wondering if things would ever get better or if Joey was right and this really was just a miserable earth.

My counselor said that eventually Joey would come around—maybe even thank me—but he never did. And it made me wonder what being a true friend actually meant. Had I messed everything up for good, breakin' the pact? But how could a true friend let things go on?

I tried asking Joey about it—tried telling him I did

what I thought a true friend ought to—but he just shook his head and kept his lips zipped.

Joey's *mama*, though, did plenty of talkin' to *my* mama, and before long Mama had convinced her to get their whole family into counseling. So Joey and his mama started going, but Joey's dad would have none of it. Said it was for sissies and women.

Well, come Christmastime, the sissies and women all packed up and left him. One afternoon after a particularly loud shoutin' match, Mrs. Banks put Joey and Rhonda in the car and just left.

They didn't come back that night, or the next, or the one after that. And since none of us had the nerve to ask Joey's dad where they'd gone, we just did a lot of speculatin' about it.

"She's probably to the Canadian border by now," Sissy said. "I'd get as far away from him as I could, that's for sure."

"Maybe she's got a relative she's staying with," Dad said.

Mama nodded. "Her mama lives near Riverdale. I bet she's gone there."

I just sat quiet. I couldn't imagine Joey living anywhere but here.

"Do you suppose they'll come back?" Sissy asked. "I don't like the thought of livin' next door to just *him*."

"I don't know what's going to happen," Mama said with a sigh. "A man's got to be willing to face himself, and I'm afraid that one's not."

It was strange living next door to only Mr. Banks. He got

a big snarling dog with fangs the size of tusks that he kept chained outside. It barked at all hours and lunged at anybody who walked by.

It was also strange because even though Joey and me hadn't talked in some time, him being gone made me feel extra lonesome. Like any hope of being friends again was gone.

By February I'd pretty much given up on ever seeing Joey again. But then one day after school, Mama greeted me at the door waving a paper in her hand. "I got a letter from them!"

"From Joey's mama?"

"Yes!"

My heart jumped clear to my throat. "Where are they? Are they comin' back? Is Joey all right?"

Mama hugged me and laughed. "They're fine! Least, fine as they can be. They're stayin' with her mama, just like I thought."

That night, Mama wrote her back, and I wrote Joey. And for the rest of the school year, I wrote Joey every couple of weeks. I hate writin', too, but it was something I did anyway. I never heard a word back from him, but Mama did hear regularly from Joey's mama, and I learned through her that Joey was still going to counseling and seemed to be doing better.

Then when the school year ended, *we* moved. Mama and Dad thought that it'd be good for me and my "quiet brooding," and good for Sissy, too. We were both having trouble finding new best friends, and they thought it'd be good to start us fresh somewhere else.

Besides, none of us were going to miss Joey's dad, especially me. He'd taken to hunting along the riverbank, which was scary enough right there. But on top of the fear of coming face to face with him, I kept having nightmares that his dog would dig up Smoky's bones.

I was all for moving, boy! All for it.

I liked the town where we moved, too. Met a kid at school who invited me over and taught me how to drive a tractor. Talk about fun! There's nothing like being in the seat of a John Deere!

'Cept maybe sliding through mud in a frog-stranglin' rain.

Anyhow, with all my new distractions, I almost quit writing Joey. But one afternoon I got an itch to do it, so I sat down and told him all about the boy next door, and how crazy he is, climbing on the roof and cock-a-doodle-dooin' every morning like a maniac rooster. I swear to howdy he's gonna try and fly someday, and when he does, I don't want to be the one to go and catch him. He's only ten, but that boy weighs two hundred pounds. Maybe three.

Then just last week Mama came in with a letter. And I could tell right off it was from Joey 'cause of the stupid stuff he'd doodled all over it. A dog liftin' its leg, a 'gator eating a barn, *flies* buzzing around all over . . . That right there busted me up, but what really made me smile was what he wrote on the front.

Rusty-boy Cooper.

I tore it open quick, and inside he wrote, "Hey-ya, Rusty-boy," and I could practically see his loopy grin again. Then he said, "So you think you're hot, having Rooster-boy next door, huh?" and went on to tell the tale of the biggest, meanest snapping turtle known to man that lives in a swamp near their house and comes out snappin' and whippin' its tail, chasin' little kids for miles.

"A turtle?" I wrote him back. "*Chasin'* folks?" Then I scribbled him the longest letter ever, tellin' him all about my new school and how I've got a teacher who stinks up the place with noisy gassers and runs a goose alongside his bike on his way to school.

Mama asked to read Joey's letter, so I let her. But when she was done, she had tears in her eyes. "What's wrong, Mama?" I asked her. "I thought it was funnier than anything!"

"It is," she told me. "I'm just so glad to see that Joey's found himself back." Then she gave me the kind of sweet look that only your mama can give you. "And I'm mighty glad for the P.S."

I was, too. It was the shortest line of the entire letter, but it meant everything to me.

"P.S. Thanks."

Mama stood up and gave me a kiss on the head. "I have

a feeling the two of you will always be bound, no matter where you go."

There's a scar on my finger that tells me that's so, and a few more inside, besides. Together they remind me what a true friend is.

And what it ain't.

ABOUT THE AUTHOR

Wendelin Van Draanen has been everything from a forklift driver to a high school teacher, but is now enjoying life as a full-time writer. She is the author of *Flipped* and the popular Sammy Keyes mystery series, the first book of which, *Sammy Keyes and the Hotel Thief*, received the 1999 Edgar Allan Poe Award for best children's mystery.

Ms. Van Draanen lives with her husband and two sons in central California. Her hobbies include the "three R's": reading, running, and rock 'n' roll.